Belmont Plantation
Virginia 1859

March 1859

The spring blooms are comin' and the sky is a sure blue. March never knows if it wants to be a spring month or a winter month. The heat's come early to Virginia this year. That's fine with me though. As long as it's hot I have to fan young mas' William and Miz Lilly, my mistress, during their study time. This mornin' was the first day of my third learnin' season. For now on three years, I been fannin' them, liftin' and lowerin' the big fan made of woven Carolina sweet grass – up and down, up and down. The fan stirs the thick air – up and down, up and down – and chases away worrisome horse flies and eye gnats. It may seem like a silly job. But, I don't mind one bit, 'cause while William is learnin', so am I.

Standin' there fannin' – up and down, up and down – I come to know my ABCs and the sounds the letters make. I teached myself how to read words. Now, I can pick through things I find to read – like throwed away newspapers, letters in the trash and books I slip off Mas' Henley's shelf. It scares me to know what I know sometimes.

Slaves aine s'posed to know how to read and write, but I

do. Miz Lilly would fall down in a fit if she knew I had made myself a diary like the one she's got on her bed table. It don't matter to me that hers is all wrapped in fine satin and got ribbons and beads on it and mine is just made up of papers I found in the trash and keeps tied together with a measure of yarn. It's a diary just the same. Mine. And I aim to write in it whenever I get a chance.

I got to be real particular and make sure nobody finds out though, 'cause if my mas'er finds out I would fall under the whip. Time and time again I done heard Mas' Henley swear that if he catches his slaves with learnin' he'll beat the skin off us, then sell our hides to slavers from the Deep South. He got the law on his side, too. Anybody found teachin' a slave in the state of Virginia can be sent to jail. Sure! Wonder why the white folks is so determined to keep us from knowin' things? What are they scared of?

Cain't help but laugh a little bit when I think of what Mas' Henley would think if he knew I could read better than his boy – and that it was his own wife that had teached me!

It's near dark. Pray Lord, don't let nobody find my diary hid behind the loose brick in the outside chimney wall, back of the kitchen. Hope it can stay dry and safe until I can sneak away to write again.

Next mornin', first light

I got up extra early and churned the butter for breakfast and helped out in the kitchen the way Aunt Tee 'spects me to every mornin'. That give me a little time to practice my writin' at my spot by the big tree out behind the kitchen. Sunrise is a good writin' hour – when all is still and quiet.

I want to tell somebody 'bout all the things I done learned for the past three years. Words got magic. Every time I read or write a word it puts a picture in my head.

Like when I write H-O-M-E I sees Belmont Plantation and all the people that live here. I sees the Big House where Mas' Henley, Miz Lilly and William stay, livin' easy. I sees the separate kitchen with the attic above it where I sleep along with Aunt Tee, Uncle Heb and Hince. I sees the Quarters where my friends live, and beyond their cabins, the fields and orchards where they work. I sees Aunt Tee cookin' at the fireplace, and the stables where Hince takes care of Mas' Henley's prize racin' horses, and the gardens and grounds that Uncle Heb makes pretty. Home. That one li'l word shows me all of that.

Mas' Henley thinks he owns everything here at Belmont,

but he don't own all of me – not really. I know, he can tell me to come and I got to come. When he say do this, I better do it or he'll put the whip to my back. But I done learned that he cain't tell me what to think – and feel – and know. He look at me every day but he cain't see what's in my head. He cain't own what's inside me. Nobody can.

Few days later

It rained all the long, long day. Everything is dampish and sticky. I wondered if my diary stayed dry in its hidin' place. No need to worry, the stone covered it well.

Next day

It rained again today. When it rains hard, the field slaves don't have to work. But our work in the kitchen goes on all the time – no days off.

Aunt Tee say I'm lucky, gettin' picked to work in the Big House. I aine so sure. Livin' right under Mas' Henley and

Miz Lilly aine so easy to me. We got to do their biddin' all hours of the night and day. But field work is hard – hard on your back, and in the summer, the heat is smothery. I guess what it comes to is bein' a slave aine no good no matter where they got you workin'.

Next day

I just wrote T-R-E-E. I see my tree – the live oak behind the kitchen where I come to write whenever I can slip away. I put a "s" on tree and now the word is trees. The picture in my head turns to the apple orchards. In spring, the apple trees are filled with bright, white blossoms. I close my eyes and see the same trees in the green of summer and full of good-tastin' apples in the fall. I love playin' with words – puttin' letters in and takin' letters out and lettin' the pictures change.

Monday

I know it's Monday, 'cause Miz Lilly comes to the kitchen every Monday mornin' to pass out the flour, sugar and meal.

It's so hard keepin' secrets from the people I live with. Sometimes when I'm helpin' Aunt Tee in the kitchen, I want to tell her 'bout my learnin' so bad. But I cain't, even though she's 'bout the closest thing to a mama I got since my own mama died five years ago. I don't think she'd do a thing to hurt me, but she been real close with Mas' Henley all his life. Been his cook – since before he got married to Miz Lilly. Cain't take the chance.

I want to tell Uncle Heb how I used his whittlin' knife to make a writin' pen out of a turkey quill. He'd be right proud of his Sunflower Girl, that's what he calls me. But he's old now, forgetful. He might just slip up and tell the wrong person, who'd tell Mas' Henley on me just to win a favour.

What I wouldn't give to tell Hince how, whilst I'm dustin', I slip ink out of Mas' Henley's study in a glass bottle. I can see him laughin' so his eyes would water up. I'd come more close to tellin' Hince my secret than anybody – him bein' like a big brother to me, always teasin' and funnin'. Hince say I study on things all the time – off by myself too much. He don't understand I aine off to myself 'cause I want to be. I'm just bein' careful-like, not wantin' to be caught practisin' my writin' and readin'.

If Mama was alive I could tell her. But Mama is gone, gone forever. Dead. So there's nobody I trust enough to tell.

Two days later

It aine even summer yet, and William is fussin' 'bout the heat. I am twelve and he is, too. But he seems so much younger. Maybe it's 'cause William is forever whinin' 'bout something – 'specially at study time. I just stay quiet and listen, fannin' – up and down, up and down. Aunt Tee say William is spoiled to a stink. Mas' Henley thinks his son is a little piece of heaven here on earth. 'Course, nobody else shares that notion, not even the boy's mama.

Next day

There's goin' to be a dinner party in the Big House tonight. Aunt Tee sent me down to the Quarters to get Aggie and Eva Mae to help out in the kitchen. Whenever I write F-R-I-E-N-D, I always put a "s" on it, 'cause I have two friends – Eva Mae's daughter, Missy. She's fifteen. And Aggie's daughter, Wook. She's sixteen. They all growed up now, but we still be friends. Known them all my life. Cain't even remember a time when I didn't know them.

I've always been a little jealous 'cause Wook and Missy be closer to each other than they's to me. And they each got their mamas with them. Missy's daddy was Mas' Henley's best jockey, but he was throwed from his horse and killed a year or so back. Now Hince do all the ridin'. Eva Mae is still grievin' and Missy misses her daddy much as I miss my mama.

Wook is lucky to have a daddy like Rufus. Anybody who knows Rufus and Aggie likes them. Rufus came to Belmont 'bout two years ago from over in Hampton. He's a strong man, big, but not fat – not tall either. Uncle Heb say he's a God-fearin' man. Mas' must have seen that Rufus was a natural-born leader, so he made Rufus the field boss.

A lot of women had their eyes on Rufus when he came, but he married Aggie, a big fine woman who had a daughter, but Rufus took Wook to be his very own daughter.

Aggie is goin' to have a baby real soon. When her time come, Aunt Tee will do the birthin'. Aunt Tee is the plantation midwife – birthed Hince, Wook, Missy and even birthed me. She look out after all the 'spectin' women. She's showed me the secrets to all her medicine recipes, but she will not let me go to a birthin' with her. I want to know 'bout such things, but Aunt Tee say, it's not for me. How do she know it's not for me, if she aine never let me go?

Next day

Even though we don't live but a short walk from each other, Wook and Missy and I don't get to visit much durin' the week – just on Saturday nights and Sunday. I got to 'fess, I likes Wook better than Missy. Missy always pushed and hit us when she was young. Now that she's a big girl, she push and hit with words. Just yesterday she come sayin' I thought I was somebody, 'cause I work in the Big House. Aggie and Wook work in the fields, hunched over all day in the hot sun. Aunt Tee say that's enough to make a body mean.

Friday

Fear of another frost is over, and the moon is full. Aunt Tee said it was time to plant the house garden behind the kitchen. The family will eat out of it all summer and well into fall. Put in greens, goobers, cabbage, okra – all we could plant on that one spot. Takin' care of the house garden is one job I don't mind doin'. Its fun workin' with the plants, watchin' them grow and make food.

Next night

It stormed earlier tonight. Flashes of lightnin' lit up the attic room. I tried not to be scared. Lord, I miss Mama. When I was little and it would storm, me and Mama would hug up close and I wouldn't be scared.

The rain has finally stopped, but it is still, hot and muggy – cain't sleep. Besides, I woke up dreamin' 'bout Mama again. I slipped quiet-like out of the kitchen, careful not to wake nobody, so I could come write.

I am here at the live oak, my spot. Here I can let my tears drop like the rain and tell the moon 'bout my sadness. Writin' 'bout my dream helps the hurt go away.

In my dream, I touched Mama's round, brown face. Like she used to do, she wet the tip of her apron and dabbed away the sweat over my upper lip and on my forehead. I saw myself readin' to her. She smiled and clapped her hands. I heared her soft voice praise me the way Mas' Henley do William when he gets the least li'l thing right.

"I knows so much more, Mama. Let me show you." The soft in her face changed and her eyes held a warnin' I couldn't understand. "What's wrong, Mama?" She wanted to say somethin', but she was pulled away into the dark by some powerful big hand. "Mama, wait." She was gone, and I woke up to the cold, hurtin' truth. Mama is dead.

Next day

I slipped off to visit with Missy and Wook today. I found them 'mongst the young tobacco plants, 'longside Rufus. I was so glad to see them. We used to have a great time together, playin' games. Then Mas' put Missy and Wook to work in the fields, and I got put to work in the Big House.

Wook's face looks tired and drawn. All Missy wanted to talk 'bout was how cute she thought Hince was. Cute? Hince? Missy got eyes for Hince? She did say somethin' that made good sense. She say that Rufus had asked Mas' Henley if he could hold a service at Eastertime. I'm surprised. Mas' aine in the habit of doin' things nice for nobody less'n it serves him.

Easter Sunday

After breakfast, we all gathered in the Quarters for the Easter meetin'. Most times all of us be so tired, we just fall out on Sunday. Try to rest. Be ready for sunrise bell come Monday. But Rufus lifted everybody's spirits today.

Mas' Henley came to the service to see what we was doin' – come talkin' 'bout how he didn't want no shoutin' and carryin' on 'bout fredum. He told us to pray for good weather and a big harvest. Sing 'bout joy and happiness. No sad songs. I wonder does he really believe we'll pray for his good fortune and not our own? He say if we do like he say, then he'll let us have more meetin's on Sunday.

Anyhow, Mas' Henley sat down, and Rufus took over. Wook tol' me once that Rufus had been the slave of a preachin' man before bein' sold to Mas' Henley. Uncle Heb say Rufus had learned the Bible from cover to cover – and know all the stories by heart. One day, I want to read the Bible for myself. There's a Bible that stays on Mas' Henley's readin' table. I've looked at it many times, but I've never touched it. I think he'd know if I did.

Rufus began the meetin' by askin' Uncle Heb to speak a prayer. Then he called on Aggie to sing. Then Rufus told us a story 'bout a brave man named Daniel who stood down lions with just his faith.

When we find ourselves in the lion's den, Rufus say that we should be like Daniel and believe that God will deliver us from all harm. Everybody shouted Amen to that, even me. But, I'm not so sure 'bout facin' a lion. What a scary thing facin' a lion.

Monday evenin'

The last meal of the day is over and all the dishes is washed. I'm so tired! "You don't know what tired is," Aunt Tee told me. "Be glad you aine got to work the fields." I cain't demagine bein' tireder than I am now. I wondered did Wook and Aggie go to bed feelin' sick-tired like me?

Day or two later

There's just enough light to practice my writin'.

Freedom is one of the first words I teached myself to write. Down in the Quarters people pray for freedom – they sing 'bout freedom, but to keep Mas' Henley from knowin' their true feelings, they call freedom "heaven." Everybody's mind is on freedom.

But it is a word that aine never showed me no picture. While fannin' this afternoon, my eyes fell on "freedom" in a book William was readin'. No wonder I don't see nothin'. I been spellin' it f-r-e-d-u-m.

I put the right letters in my head to make sure I remembered their place. F-R-E-E-D-O-M. I just now wrote it. Still no picture. Nothin'. The letters just sit there on the page. Spelled right or wrong, freedom got no picture, no magic. Freedom is just a word.

Friday

Whenever I dust Mas' Henley's study I look at his calendar and get the date. Today is Friday, April 1, 1859.

First Sunday in April

'Round here, they don't work the field hands on Sunday, but us who works in the kitchen and Big House, don't get but a few hours off on Sunday mornin' and in the evenin' after the last meal is served. We didn't even get that much time off today.

A new girl named Spicy come to the kitchen today. She's got 'bout fifteen years. Miz Lilly bought her from the Ambrose Plantation. S'posed to help Aunt Tee and me with the cookin' and cleanin'. I'm glad she's here. We need all the help we can get. But Aunt Tee aine so happy. She thinks Spicy is a spy for Miz Lilly.

"Clotee, make sure you don't give Spicy no bones to take to the Big House."

It's a fair warnin'. Mas' Henley and Miz Lilly promise us extra clothin' and sweets if we tell them things. The Missus promised to give me a handkerchief with yellow and purple pansies at each corner if I told her things 'bout what went on here in the kitchen. I wouldn't tell her nothin' if she promised me a box full of handkerchief. None of us in the kitchen are tattlers. I hope Spicy aine one either.

Later the same day

Spicy seems nice enough. Quiet though. We got her settled in and ready to start work come daybreak Monday, here in Aunt Tee's kitchen.

"Our day starts when the roosters crow," say Aunt Tee.

It made me dizzy listenin' to her put to words all the things we do 'round here. We fix three meals every day – take the food up to the Big House and serve it. Miz Lilly likes her food served on time. First meal is on the table at 8 o'clock. Midday meal is served up at noon. Dinner is at 6.30 o'clock. Then we clean up and get ready for the next day. In between, we do general house cleanin' – dustin'. Miz Lilly wants a clean house, but she aine willin' to help keep it clean – throw stuff all 'round in her room, dresser all messy. We wash on Monday and iron on Tuesday. Eva Mae and Aggie come up from the Quarters to help out on those days.

"William don't eat at the table with his folks," Aunt Tee say. "He eats at a smaller table to the side an hour 'fore his folks. You'll serve him. You understand, girl?"

Spicy shook her head yes. I aine never seen nobody with eyes that look like big pools of sorryness. I wonder what's done happened to Spicy to make her look so sad?

Monday

It's Monday again. Miz Lilly come swishin' to the kitchen first thing this mornin', measurin' out the flour, sugar and so on. Actin' like she know what's goin' on. "That woman don't know salt from sugar," Aunt Tee chuckled under her breath, "let alone how to cook with it." But the Missus likes to pr'tend that she's in charge of the kitchen, but we all know better. Ask anybody and they'll tell you Aunt Tee is the mistress of Belmont's kitchen.

Miz Lilly counts the cans of perserves and the dried vegetables 'gainst the recipes, makin' sure we don't eat extra food or give it away to the people in the Quarters. In the

19

Quarters, they don't never get enough to eat or enough time to eat it.

But Aunt Tee been cookin' here at Belmont since Mas' Henley married Miz Lilly sixteen years ago. She was the onlyest slave he owned when he come here. Everybody else b'longed to Miz Lilly's family. They was the one's rich. Mas'er come from Tennessee, po' as a church mouse, but he wooed the widow Lilly until she married him. Aunt Tee say Mas'er married the money and not Miz Lilly. He was hopin' that if'n he owned Belmont it would make him a gentleman. He aine no gentleman though, no matter how much money he got.

Aunt Tee got her own way of doin' things in the kitchen, and it makes Miz Lilly mad. "I aine 'bout to cook and not eat," say Aunt Tee, laughin'. She knows how to pinch and save back, so we most times got a-plenty to eat. Sometime, she skims off enough to slip food to a sick child or a nursin' mother in the Quarters. What we're all hopin' is that Spicy can be trusted not to tattle.

I don't know for sure, but I don't think Spicy is a tattler. She aine talkin' much to nobody. So we just been leavin' her be.

Monday again

Spicy been here a week, already. She's as big as a man and just 'bout as strong. But Lord that girl is clumbsy. She's forever stumblin' over things, droppin' things and knockin' over things.

"She been used to hard work," Aunt Tee say, with a little less suspicion in her voice. Spicy got on the good side of Aunt Tee when she helped wring the water out of big ol' heavy sheets like they was just hand towels and never once complained – even when her hands was all red and sore. Spicy can lift hot pots and even chop wood. Her hands is rough, but even so, she's right pretty. Hard to get a look at her square on,'cause she holds her head down all the time.

She's older than me and bigger than me. For some reason, though, I feel like she needs takin' care of. Maybe it's her sad eyes that make me feel that way.

Later

"That gal b'longs in the fields," say Mas' Henley when he saw Spicy servin' the table with me.

"She'll be a great help here in the house," say Miz Lilly. Say she bought her for a little of nothin'.

Spicy don't know it yet, but she's in the middle of a big mess here at Belmont. Mas' Henley and Miz Lilly always be on the two ends of a stick. One say up – the other is bound to say down. Miz Lilly bought Spicy, so Mas' Henley is sure to find fault with her.

It goes like that all the time – them two havin' silly fights 'bout one thing or another. Miz Lilly say Aunt Tee is uppity and needs a good beatin'. Mas' don't like Uncle Heb. Say he's useless. "Diggin' 'round out there in them roses don't put meat in my storehouse." He cain't see that Belmont is a pretty place 'cause Uncle Heb cares so much 'bout the flowers. Mas' Henley cain't see pretty 'cause he's too mean inside.

If mean was a tree, it would grow tall here at Belmont.

Tuesday

Durin' lesson time, the Missus gave William a smack on his ear. "And you, Clotee! Come closer," she snapped at me, as if I had somethin' to do with the heat. "Move that fan faster." But that's 'xactly what I wanted her to say. Move closer. Standin' directly behind William, I can look over his shoulder and see the words in his book.

Sometimes when I'm fannin', I make out like I done fell asleep – I let my arms drop. Then when Miz Lilly yells at me, I jump like I'm wakin' up. This makes her think I'm not interested in what's goin' on.

I have to be careful doin' that though. I don't want to get caught learnin', but I don't want to lose my job neither.

Next day

The noon meal was broke up when twenty riders stopped by Belmont lookin' for a man what they say is a northern abo –

somethin' I aine never heared before. The compression on Mas' Henley's face say to me that whatever he is, the man is in deep trouble.

Mas' Henley sent Hince to ring the plantation bell, callin' everybody to the front of the house. Mas' counted heads to make sure all 27 of us was there. He showed 'round a drawin' of a white man with a tangle of dark hair. He had a patch over his left eye.

"You ever see this man, you come straight and tell me. I'll make it sweet for whoever helps us catch him." He looked at the picture, spat, then crumpled it into a ball and throwed it away. Again, he called the man an abo-abolistine, I think.

When no one was lookin' I picked up the crumpled-up piece of paper and hid it under my dress. I want to know what this abolistine is.

Thursday

Spicy and I helped Aunt Tee make ginger cakes. Spicy spilled more than she got in the bowl. She's just natural-born clumbsy. Right after the last meal, Hince and Uncle Heb come to the kitchen for dinner.

Aunt Tee had fixed a two layer cake with strawberry perserves in the middle for Mas' Henley, or at least he thought it was for him. Aunt Tee had saved out just enough batter to make me a little cake 'bout the size of my hand. She say, "A bird flew by and told me there's a girl livin' 'round here who's been in this world near 'bout twelve years."

Nobody knows the real day I was borned, but Aunt Tee say, "You come here when the dogwoods bloomed."

"Yo' mama loved the very breath you took. All us did," say Uncle Heb. He handed me a doll he'd carved out of hardwood, no larger than two thumbs.

I've named her Little Bit, 'cause she so small. Mama knew Aunt Tee and Uncle Heb. In fact when she got sent away, she put me in their care. That all happened when I had just come to the age of rememberin'.

Hince made me a sun hat out of field grasses, and put it on my head. He had to tease me 'bout it, sayin', "If you lose it, I'm gon' bus' yo' head."

These words seemed to upset Spicy somethin' fierce. She snatched off her apron and ran out the door. I started to go after her – tell her Hince didn't mean it. He wouldn't hit me. "Let her be," said Aunt Tee. So we did.

Spicy is totin' a basket full of sorrow on her head. Been beat down so much, I 'spect. When somebody raise they hand, she covers her head. Mostly I been lettin' her be. She don't say much, so I don't say much back to her. At night when we lay side by side on our sleepin' pallets, I can hear her cryin'. I wonder can she hear me cryin' sometime, too?

Friday

Seen Mas' Henley's calendar today. It's Friday, April 15, 1859. Been practisin' my writin', too. I just wrote R-I-V-E-R. I sees the James River out in front of the Big House. Wonder what's down that ol' lazy, movin' river? I aine never been away from Belmont. Maybe one day Miz Lilly will take me 'long with her when she goes to Richmond to shop and visit.

Saturday

This mornin' Hince and Spicy got into the worse spat. She's real touch-ous 'bout her name being Spicy. Hince found out, and that was good for a tease. He asked if Spicy was more cinnamon or more nutmeg? Lord, what did he say that for! Spicy hauled off and whacked him right in the mouth.

"You half-white dog," she screamed at him. Hince went sprawlin' out on the ground.

"You addled, girl?" he shouted back. Hurt took over his face. None of us ever say much 'bout the way he looks. Spicy's eyes filled with tears and she stomped off in a huff, sayin', "You might look like ol' mas'er, but you aine really white. And I aine got to put up with you devilin' me!"

Words said cain't be taken back – even if they is true. Hince could pass for anybody's ordinary white boy – a member of the Big House family. He's got grayish-lookin' cat eyes and curly, sandy hair. There's talk in the Quarters that his daddy is a white man – Mas' Henley's brother, maybe, or even Mas' Henley, hisself. I don't care who his daddy is. Hince is like my brother and I know it bothers him that he looks white, but he is black.

Later

Whenever I'm troubled 'bout somethin', I go find Uncle Heb in the roses and help him weed. 'Fore I know it, the troubles don't seem so bad.

I told Uncle Heb 'bout what Spicy said. "Colour of yo' skin don't matter when you're a slave," Uncle Heb s'plained to me real easy-like. "Virginia law say, if the mama be black, then her chir'ren be black. If the mama be a slave, then her chir'ren be a slave. Hince looks white but he's black 'cause his mama Ola was black. Never mind who his daddy be."

Aunt Tee never say who Hince's daddy is, and I dare not ask. Cain't help but wonder though. Does Hince know who his daddy really is? And if it is Mas' Henley, then, how do it make him feel, bein' the slave of his own daddy? There's somethin' deep down wrong 'bout such a thing. But it go on all the time. Lots of white-lookin' black folks live in the Quarters. They's daddys be white, but they mamas be slaves. So they be slaves, too. Aine right!

I aine never seen my daddy. Mama told me his name was Bob Coleman. He drowned in the river 'fore I was borned. We all live right here on the river, but cain't none of us swim. Mas' won't 'llow it – say we run away. Thinkin' 'bout my daddy makes me think 'bout my mama. I miss Mama so bad it hurts 'cause I knew her, touched her face, seen her smile. But in a strange way I miss my daddy, too, even though I aine never, ever saw him.

Midweek

Sunshine skies, blue skies so far this week. Spicy and me been piecin' a quilt 'bout a hour or two every night – patches from old rags the Missus throwed away. Aunt Tee is always busy scrubbin' old pots with river sand, or shellin' or snappin' some kind of bean. If Uncle Heb aine down in the stables with Hince or drivin' the family to or from somewhere, he sits with us. We tell stories to pass the time.

My favourite story is how Uncle Heb and Aunt Tee got married.

Uncle Heb starts the tale, but Aunt Tee puts in along the way. When Aunt Tee got to Belmont, Uncle Heb was livin' here over the kitchen where she was put to live. She caught his eye right away, she bein' so fine-lookin' and all. "She put me in the mind of you, Spicy, but she was real skinny. Didn't weigh more than one hundred pounds soakin' wet. I says to her for fun one day, 'How can you be a good cook thin as you is?'"

Aunt Tee took one look at Heb, and says to Mas' Henley, "I aine gon' live in sin with no man, never-you-mind how old he is." And she just wouldn't cook for a day or two.

Uncle Heb picks up the story again. Miz Lilly was put out. In her mind, slaves stayed where they was put, and that was that. Left up to her, Aunt Tee woulda got a good beatin' for havin' the nerve to rebel. But Mas' Henley is particular 'bout who fixes his food. Aunt Tee done been with him for years. When Miz Lilly tried to get one of the women from the Quarters to cook, he wouldn't 'llow it.

Finally, Mas' come upon a perfect salvation that was good for everybody – 'specially Uncle Heb. One Sunday mornin' durin' the Christmas Big Times, the preacher man come to Belmont. "Mas' announced that Aunt Tee and me was to jump the broom."

"Didn't ask us. Just told us," said Aunt Tee. "I wouldn't have chose this old man, myself," she always say, smilin'. "But over time, I done warmed to the idea of havin' him 'round though."

"Come Christmas it will be our sixteenth year together," Uncle Heb say. At that point, Aunt Tee always pats him on the back of his hand. That's the way the story always ends, everybody smilin'. Them smilin' at each other. I love that story and the way they tell it. It makes me feel good all the way through and through.

Friday

The days is gettin' longer, and that means we have to work longer, too. In the summer, Miz Lilly bath almost every day. This evenin', Spicy and me carried water up the steps in buckets and poured it in Miz Lilly's bathin' tub. Then when she got through, we had to drain the water into buckets and take them down the steps and dump it. Spicy spilled water all up and down the steps comin' and goin'. I got tickled at her, and she got tickled at herself. 'Fore you know it, we was laughin' so hard. It felt fine to laugh. And it felt even finer to see Spicy laughin'. I didn't think she knew how.

Next night

It's a clear night. Good moon. Good night to write.

The upper room was too stuffy to sleep, so I brought my mat outside. We sometimes do that. Spicy followed me. It was just the two of us girls. We just laid there, lookin' up at the stars. We had laughed together, so it was easier for us to talk together.

Come to find out, Spicy is motherless, too. And, just as I thought, she been mistreated somethin' awful – beaten and yelled at by her ol' mas'. Say he's meaner than Mas' Henley. I cain't demagine.

"If I could, I'd run away from this place so far they'd never fine me," she blurted out, lookin' like a cornered cat. "You won't tell on me, will you?"

"None of us is tattlers," I told her.

"I aine either," she said. I believe her.

Fourth Sunday in April

Sunrise will be here soon, but before startin' the day, I want to write "freedom" again. It is such a strong word to so many people. F-R-E-E-D-O-M. Freedom. No picture comes to my mind. It just aine got the magic. It shows me nothin'.

I've looked at the drawin' of the one-eyed man over and over. His face don't show me nothin' neither. One thing for sure – if the one-eyed man is doin' somethin' that makes Mas' Henley mad, then I figure he cain't be all that bad.

Monday

Miz Lilly favours her daughter Clarissa and I see why. She's all growed up and married with children of her own near 'bout the same age as William. Aunt Tee say Miz Lilly thought she was through havin' babies, when along come William. She almost up and died tryin' to get him borned. If it hadn't been for Aunt Tee they say Miz Lilly would have done died. The fancy doctors from over in Richmond had done everythin', but Aunt Tee fixed up a potion and the next mornin', little William come into this world feet first.

"The tree with all its won-won-won" William was tryin' to read a poem and got stuck on a easy word. His face turned all red. "What's it say, Mama?"

Miz Lilly is short tempered and quick to hit in good times. Today wasn't one of her better days. She whacked William's knuckles with a stick. "Wonderful!" she shouted. "Wonderful. That's a plain English word used by millions of people. Wonderful. Look at it. Say it. Won-der-ful!"

William threw the book over his shoulder and stomped away. Miz Lilly followed close behind, threatenin' to skin him alive. The lessons ended on that sour note.

I looked in the hedges and found the book William had tossed away. I'll give it back to the Missus in a bit, but not before I've had a chance to finish readin' the rest of that poem.

Tuesday

Wonder what a new pair of shoes feels like? It's warm enough to go barefooted now. My feet are glad to be out of William's old throwed away shoes. The ground feels good comin' up through my toes all soft and cushy-like. Maybe that's how new shoes feel.

Wednesday

Mr Ben Tomson's Betty came to Belmont to finish fittin' a dress for the Missus. Betty is a good seamtress. Her mas'er hires her out to make clothes for people far away. Makes weddin' dresses, fancy party dresses – everythin'. Good as she is, though, Betty cain't hold a candle to my mama when she was the seamtress. Here at Belmont. Everybody say so.

The ugliest dress in Virginia is bein' made right here at Belmont for Miz Lilly. It is a shade of light green that looks washed out – no colour. I'd rather wear this little plain cotton shirt I got on, with nothin' underneath it, than all that grand mess she's havin' made.

After Betty finished in the Big House, she stopped by to speak to Aunt Tee in the kitchen. I listened, careful not to jump into grown folk's talk.

Betty say Jasper and Naomi from over at the Teasdale Plantation runned away several weeks ago! The dogs was on they cents, when all of a sudden, they got all befuddled – went to howlin' and carryin' on.

"Heared red pepper will do that," say Aunt Tee.

Then Betty say somethin' that make me listen real close. "Word tell, it was a white man that helped them get 'way on a railroad what runs under the ground – a one-eyed white man, they says."

That set me to thinkin'. If the one-eyed man helped Jasper and Naomi run 'way then he must be what they calls a abolistine.

Day later

I cain't stop thinkin' 'bout the abolistines. Seems some white folks don't want slavery. They be the abolistines. I can hardly demagine that – but it makes me happy to know that them kind of people is out there somewhere. The white folks that is mas'ers wants to keep slavery. I know 'bout them. I want to know more 'bout the abolistines. Where do they live? How many is it? Do they all wear patches over their eyes? Are they all men? One thing for sure is that the abolistines is helpin' slaves to get to freedom, and knowin' that is good for now.

Friday evenin', April 29, 1859 (I think)

Spicy and I was dustin' the large parlour. Spicy broke a vase and Miz Lilly gave her a bad whuppin' – ten hard swats across the back with a switch – look more like a tree limb to me.

Aunt Tee rubbed her wounds with a paste made from powdered oak leaves and rain water. Takes the sting out and keeps the sores from festerin'. It almost made me sick when I saw Spicy's back. It wasn't the new cuts, but the old scars. She done been beat many, many times before – and hard, too. Now, I see why Spicy is so deep down hurt – been beat on so much. I aine never come under the lash like that, and I don't want to either. Miz Lilly beat Spicy bad just for breakin' a vase. What would she do to me if she knew I could read and write? The idea makes me tremble.

Sunday – after last meal

I almost died of fear when Spicy spilled gravy on a guest's dress, broke a plate and chipped a cup while servin' dinner. I thought Miz Lilly was goin' to kill her. Miz Lilly promised her guests: "She's goin' straight to the tobacco fields tomorrow." I saw Spicy smile. She wanted to get sent to the fields – to get away from bein' 'round Mas' Henley and Miz Lilly. That was a silly way to go 'bout it, and I told her so, later on. Anyway, Spicy's plan didn't work. 'Cause just to spite his wife, Mas' Henley took sides with Spicy. Say all Spicy needs is to be trained.

"Why do you care what happens to me?" Spicy asked me later.

"I saw your back and I wouldn't want that to happen to you again – not to nobody! And I like you—" Spicy looked real surprised – like nobody had ever said that to her before.

So for now, Spicy stays with us in the kitchen. And I'm glad. I think she might be, too.

First Sunday in May

Cooked and served three meals. Two house guests. Toted waters for baths. Helped with the clean up. I am so tired. No spirit to write. I've still got to wash out my dress, so I'll start the week clean.

Monday night

Aunt Tee sent me down to the Quarters to take a ointment to Aggie. Spicy went 'long. Wook tries to be nice. But for some reason, Missy done took a dislikin' to Spicy. That Missy is really changin'. I showed her Little Bit, and she laughed at me 'bout still playin' with dolls. Later, Spicy told me not to worry 'bout what Missy say. "People teases you sometimes 'cause they know it'll make you mad."

I asked her why she let Hince's teasin' make her so mad then?

"I hate my name," she say. "Spicy! Whoever heared of such a silly name? My mama was all set to call me Rose. But our ol' mistress say no, and named me Spicy. Mama had to do it – couldn't say nothin' 'bout it."

The more I learn 'bout Spicy the more I like her, but the more I hurt deep down for her, too.

Day later

Hince hardly ever comes to the kitchen since he and Spicy had that bad fallin' out. So, I been goin' to the stables whenever I get a chance. "Is Spicy mean to you?" Hince asked me.

"Not at all." I told him Spicy is just totin' a lot of hurt from the way she been treated. He nodded a understandin'. I really do like her a lot. I think she might be my friend. I wrote F-R-I-E-N-D-S. This time I seen Hince, Wook and now Spicy. Missy aine even now in the picture.

Wednesday

Hince and Mas' Henley been goin' to horse races most every week. They rode off last night, on the way to Southampton. Hince is a mighty fine jockey – wins a heap of money for Mas' Henley.

Wednesday evenin'

I can smell the word K-I-T-C-H-E-N and see it, too. It always smells good – herbs hangin' from the eaves, dryin'. Hickory chips slow-burnin' on the back fire. A pot bubblin' or boilin'. Aunt Tee loves her big, four-hip fireplace where four grown women can stand side by side and cook together. She's truly the mistress of Belmont's kitchen.

Miz Lilly was in the kitchen today chatterin' on 'bout what she wanted fixed for a special dinner. Aunt Tee just say, "Yes, Miz Lilly," but in the end, Aunt Tee cooked what she always fixes on Wednesday.

I had to tell Spicy how Aunt Tee and Mas' Henley get along. Mas' Henley be real particular 'bout what goes in his mouth. He don't trust nobody but Aunt Tee to fix his food. I once heared him say, he wouldn't eat behind a cook he had to beat – scared of bein' poisoned, I s'pose. Aunt Tee know just who she cooks for, and it aine Miz Lilly. "Mas' 'spects to have fried chicken and whipped potatoes on Wednesdays and that's what I fixed." And that's what we served to the guests tonight.

Next day

Tellin' Spicy the way things work here at Belmont is fun. Last night I 'splained to her why Mas' Henley favours Aunt Tee, but all the time 'gainst Uncle Heb. The best way for her to get an understandin' was to start at the beginnin' – back when Mas' Henley first come to Belmont.

Uncle Heb was here at Belmont when Mas' Henley married Miz Lilly who was a widow-woman with one child. Uncle Heb ran the place, keepin' the orchards goin' and all.

Word tell, Uncle Heb was once a tall, handsome man. Even now, all crippled from hard work and age, he still look good. First thing when he got here, Mas' Henley wanted to sell Uncle Heb. Miz Lilly wouldn't have it. Uncle Heb had been born here at Belmont. Him and Miz Lilly's daddy, David Monroe, was boys together. Miz Lilly likes to brag that presidents and governors have ate here at Belmont.

Uncle Heb loves to brag, too. "Been all over this 'Merican land," he say, callin' up memories of when he travelled 'round with David Monroe. He say he been everywhere. "Take the time me and the Mas'er went to Richmond Norfolk ... Jamestown ... even been to Mount Vernon. Been everywhere, all over this big 'Merican country." I would give anythin' to see just one of them places.

Hince is the onlyest one of us who done travelled further than Uncle Heb. I remember once, William told me there were ghosts in the woods and a big snake lived there. It ate up all slaves who dared to leave Belmont. It was Uncle Heb who taught me better. Everybody young and old loves the old man – everybody 'cept'n Mas' Henley – and that's 'cause he's part of Miz Lilly's family. "Mas' Henley aine nothin' but white trash who married into a fine Virginia family," say Uncle Heb. He's never had no use for his new master.

Saturday

There was a gatherin' down in the barn tonight, 'cause Wook jumped the broom with Lee – a man from the Teasdale Plantation – near 'bout twice Wook's age. Mas' Henley came down to the party and said a few words 'bout wantin' them to have lots and lots of babies.

I cain't believe Wook is married. She's only a few years older than me – and I aine near 'bout ready to be married. And by the look on Wook's face she aine ready neither. I didn't even know she was lookin' at boys. Now, she's married – and I didn't even know it. Why didn't she tell me?

All of us from the kitchen were there. Spicy came, even though she didn't want to. Uncle Heb cut roses for each one of us to put in our hair. I took the red one and Spicy liked the yellow one. She looks happier than when she came here, but her eyes still hold a lot of sorry.

Hince got back. He was there, dancin' with all the girls. The only man that aine married here at Belmont is Hince. Everybody's wonderin' who will Hince jump the broom with? The way Missy been lookin' at him, I think she'd say yes to him today. But Hince can do better than Missy. I sure hope so.

Hince does know how to have a good time. Ever since I can remember he's danced with me first. Tonight, he passed right by and asked Spicy to dance first. I was surprised and a bit put-out. I 'spose it was his way of makin' up to her. I didn't think Spicy would dance with him – but I was wrong.

When she stood up, everybody started gigglin'. Everybody knows how clumbsy Spicy can be. But she fooled us all, kickin' up her heels and pattin' the juba better than anybody 'round here had seen before.

I saw a side of Spicy I didn't know was there. She was happy, smilin' big, light-footed, free as a bird. Spicy wasn't clumbsy at all when she was dancin'. Lookin' at Hince and her turnin' together, made me forget that I was mad at Hince for not dancin' with me first. It was all right.

After that dance, everybody was askin' Spicy to cut a pigeon wing or shoo fly. Nobody asked me to dance. Even if they did, Aunt Tee wouldn't let me, 'cause she say I'm not courtin' age yet. Just Hince, 'cause he's like a brother.

It was such a good party – but I don't think Wook enjoyed one minute of it. She just sat with her arms folded, lookin' sad. If she didn't want to get married, why did she?

Sunday

Hince came to worship service for the first time this mornin'. Only 'cause Aunt Tee made him. He sat between Spicy and me and made faces, tryin' to make us laugh. Aunt Tee pinched me on the arm to make me behave. All the time Missy rolled her eyes at us. Then afterwards, we all had to hurry back to get supper on the table. But Missy jumped in front of Spicy. "Jus' 'cause you up in the Big House with the white folks, don't mean you gon' get to marry Hince. He gon' jump the broom with me, so don't you be lookin' at him, you hear?" And she strutted away.

Hince aine thinkin' 'bout jumpin' the broom with nobody. Missy just wanted to say somethin' mean to Spicy. But I cain't help but think – Spicy and Hince? Now that's a match I wouldn't have put together. But the more I think 'bout it, and remember them dancin' together – the better I like the idea. Spicy and Hince.

Monday

I been learnin' a lot durin' study time. I know the seasons, the days of the week, the months and the order they come in. Mostly, we tell time by the sun, the moon and what's happenin' on that day. The rains have set in and it's hard to tell one day from the next – just grayness. No sun. Everythin' I touch feels dampish.

Tuesday

Wook waved at me from the fields. I waved back. Aunt Tee say I cain't keep company with Wook any more, 'cause she's a married woman. "Girls and women ought not to mingle."

When I write Wook's name, I sees her bein' a growed-up woman with a husband. A part of me wants to be round and full like Wook, or maybe a little bit wild and pretty like Missy, or even tall and strong-lookin' like Spicy. But I aine none of those things. But if I could be – I'd like to be just a little bit pretty.

I've looked at myself in Miz Lilly's mirror before. I aine what you call homely, but I'd like for my teeth not to be so big. My head sits square on my shoulders, but I'd like to be taller – stronger. I guess I'm all right, but I don't feel all right.

Wednesday

It was durin' the dark of night when Rufus came knockin' at the kitchen door, hollerin' and all in a sweat. Aggie was 'bout to give birth. I begged Aunt Tee to let me go with her durin' the birthin', but she aine never let me go and she didn't this time neither. She took Spicy. I was mad and sat in a huff. Big girls got to do all kinds of things. I wasn't little any more and I wasn't a growed up woman. I was somethin' in between.

I fumed and fussed until they got back, and I made Spicy tell me everythin' – everythin'. Aunt Tee was right. Midwifein' aine for me. I don't think I ever want to see a baby bein' birthed – not after what Spicy say went on. But I looked close at the smile on Spicy's face while she was tellin' me that Rufus and Aggie had a big, healthy boy. "And I helped to get him here," she say real excited-like. Spicy had light in her eyes. I heard happy in her voice, and I knew Aunt Tee was right to take Spicy along.

Next day

All I can think 'bout today is that Aggie and Rufus have now made Mas' Henley the owner of 28 slaves. Their little baby don't belong to them – he belongs to Mas' Henley.

Followin' day

I went to see the new baby today. I picked a bunch of wildflowers to take to Aggie. Aunt Tee sent a basket of good things she had been holdin' back for Aggie to eat 'cause she's nursin' and needs the nourishmentation.

Wook showed me her new baby brother. It felt so good to hold him – so soft. Aggie and Rufus be so proud. I see why. Their baby boy is so beautiful. Aunt Tee seen to it that Mas' Henley 'llows new mothers a week free from the fields after havin' a baby. Aggie will get to be with her son for a whole week – just him and her.

I finally got a chance to talk to Wook and I found out

about her gettin' married. Like I suspicioned, Wook hates bein' married. But Mas' Henley made her marry Lee. See, Miz Lilly keeps up with the girls who come of age, and she tells Mas' Henley. When Wook turned fifteen, he told her to choose a husband. When she didn't, he picked out Lee – said they'd make strong babies. "Lee don't love me," she said. "And I don't love him. This aine no marriage."

"Aunt Tee and Uncle Heb didn't love each other when they got married, but they grew to, later on. Maybe you and Lee will come to care 'bout each other." I didn't believe what I was sayin' and neither did Wook. How can they, when they don't even-now live together? Lee can only get passes once in a while.

Is that goin' to happen to me? When I come of age, is Mas' Henley gon' make me marry somebody just so I can have babies for him to own? I won't let that happen to me. I won't.

Saturday

All week we been busy cleanin' the Big House. Winter dirt been scrubbed away to make room for summer dust. We've all worked until our hands be raw and our backs ache. Aunt Tee made a salve to help the soreness. She makes me watch when she's makin' up stuff. I know the recipes to all kinds of salves and potions, but she done forbidden me to tell anyone her secrets. It makes me feel bad sometimes that Aunt Tee tells me her secrets, 'cause I'm scared to tell her mine.

Later on

An old gamblin' friend of Mas' Henley's, Stanley Graves, been here for a day or so. Miz Lilly been takin' her meals with William. Not that she wanted to, but to spite Mas' Henley. She don't 'prove of his gamblin'.

While Spicy and me was a-servin' dessert, we overheard Graves and Mas' talkin' about abolistines. I listened to as much as I dared. Graves say they think the abolistines might run a man for president of the United States. I know 'bout the president from study time. He's the mas'er of all the other mas'ers. If the president is a abolistine, then he can do 'way with slavery and the mas'ers can't stop him.

I heared a new word. Cecession. I'm gon' add it to my list of words to know.

Third Sunday in May

I read the calendar on Mas' Henley's desk. It is Sunday, May 22, 1859. Rufus talked 'bout the Garden of Eden this mornin'. God's garden, filled with peace, love, no hurt, no sufferin' and no slavery. There aine no such place 'round here and that's for sure. All through service we could hear Mas' Henley and Miz Lilly fightin' again – shoutin' mean words, flyin' every which way. That means it's gon' be hard on Spicy and me when we have to 'tend her. She just as soon slap us for bein' in the room as to not.

After Sunday late meal, I came here to write in my special spot. I just wrote B-O-A-T, and I sees a boat full of people sailin' past Belmont on their way somewhere. I wave at them. They wave back. Wonder are they thinkin' 'bout me the way I'm thinkin' 'bout them? Wonder are there any abolistines on that boat?

Days later

Rained all yesterday and today – no scary thunder and lightnin' – just a steady drip, drip, drop. Been so damp, mould is creepin' up the side of the kitchen walls. We spent the mornin' scrubbin' the walls down with vinegar water.

After last meal, Aunt Tee sent Spicy down to the stables with Hince's dinner. She come back just a-smilin'. "Well, I do declare," say Aunt Tee, lookin' real surprised. "I b'lieve Spicy is sweet on Hince."

Aunt Tee is 'bout the last one to catch on. Everybody's talkin' 'bout how the two of them been lookin' at each other in that special way. I knew it since the party. Spicy and Hince. Spicy is a different person from when she come here. Different in a good way. Spicy and Hince. That Missy is 'bout to have a cat fit. Good.

Next afternoon

It's Thursday. I shall never forget this day. William almost caught me readin'. Lordy, I got to be more careful. I was dustin' Mas' Henley's study where there are all manner of books. I found one called an Atlas. I was so excited to find out it was a book filled with maps. I was lookin' for Virginia, when, all at once, the door flew open, and William walked in.

William laughed real wicked-like. "I know what you were doin'," he said. "You was readin' that book!"

I thought I would die when he called his mama. My tongue got thick and my throat felt dry when I thought 'bout what was goin' to happen to me. Miz Lilly came runnin' from the large parlour, answerin' William's call. "Mother, Clotee was readin'," William said. "She was in here with the door shut. I caught her readin'," and he laughed and laughed.

I stood there with my head down, lookin' as blank-faced as I could. Miz Lilly made William stop tormentin' me. "I thought you called me about somethin' serious. Where would Clotee learn how to read?" she said. Her petticoats swished as she walked away. "Keep the door open, Clotee," say Miz Lilly, turnin' to look back at me, real curious-like.

William had been just funnin'. He went on laughin', but my knees was still shakin'.

Saturday

Aunt Tee said her elbow hurt all night, so it was goin' to rain 'fore nightfall. I don't know why it should surprise me. Aunt Tee's elbow is good at callin' the weather. But, the almanack I seen in Mas' Henleys study said the May of 1859 was goin' to be wet.

I found out 'bout an almanack the same way I found out 'bout the atlas, just by dustin' the bookshelves in Mas' Henley's study.

At first, I couldn't believe that somebody could know ahead when the moon was goin' to be full. But, sure enough, the moon was full on the very day the almanack say it would be.

Now, I've got to be very careful lookin' through Mas' Henley's books, gettin' answers to my questions. After almost gettin' caught, I'm real nervous-like.

Monday

The sun is still up, even though the time of day is late. Miz Lilly has changed the study time to early in the mornin' when it's cool. I'm still s'posed to fan.

Hince and William went for a mornin' ride, makin' William late. Miz Lilly pitched a fit. Sooner or later all of us gets on the bad side of Miz Lilly, but Hince can't do nothin' to please her. Good thing Hince comes under Mas' Henley's say so. Hince would have it hard if he had to work with Miz Lilly. He knows it and stays 'way from her most of the time, too. Word tell, Miz Lilly hates Hince on account of his mama Ola and the talk that goes on 'bout Mas' Henley bein' the boy's father.

Aunt Tee is real closed-mouthed 'bout it all. But from what I can pick up here and there from the women in the Quarters, Miz Lilly wouldn't rest 'till Hince's mama was sold. Say Ola was just too pretty. Miz Lilly would-a sold Hince, too, but Mas' Henley put his foot down on that. Say a male slave would bring more money when he got older and been trained. Mas' Henley promised Miz Lilly he would keep Hince 'til he was at least sixteen.

At first frost, Hince will come into his sixteenth year. Wonder will Miz Lilly 'member the promise? I hope not. I wouldn't want nothin' bad to happen to my brother-friend Hince.

Tuesday

Thinkin' 'bout Hince's mama always puts me to thinkin' 'bout my own, 'cause they was sold one shortly after the other. Longer days allow me more chances to write. I just wrote M-A-M-A. Mama. I see her the way I seen her last – a dark-faced woman with joyedly eyes. Then the bad lonesome feelin' comes into my heart – memories that sour in my heart. No more writin' this night.

Wednesday

I didn't know I was walkin' 'round lookin' so sad, 'til Spicy said somethin'. While pluckin' chickens for the dinner meal, I told her 'bout Mama.

I told her 'bout how my mama got caught in the never-endin'

fight that goes on in the Big House 'tween Mas' Henley and Miz Lilly.

Soon after Ola was sold, Mas' Henley gave Mama 'way to his sister and brother-in-law, Amelia and Wallace Morgan, as a weddenin' present. Since Mama was a good dressmaker, she could bring good money into their house. I was a baby and not part of the deal. Aunt Tee say Miz Lilly was so mad, when she found out Mama had been gave 'way. Say she turned purple – no doubt worried 'bout who was gon' make her dresses.

The madder Miz Lilly got, the more set in his way Mas' Henley got. "You made me get rid of Ola, now you've got to let Rissa go." That brought 'bout a faintin' spell, the kind Miz Lilly gets when she's tryin' to win a point. All her fallin' out couldn't save Mama. She had to go to Richmond.

Later

The night before Mama was taken away, she gave me to Aunt Tee and Uncle Heb. When Uncle Heb retells it, he say it was right after the Big Times – the first of the year. "Clotee is yours now. Take care of her, love her if you can," she tol' them.

I only got to see Mama, a few times after that – once when

Wallace and Amelia come to Belmont and brought her 'long to take care of their baby. Then durin' the Christmas holiday she got a pass to come visit. Each time she came, we laughed and talked, cried and held each other. She always waited 'til I fell asleep, then she'd leave. When I woke up, Mama would be gone . . . just gone.

Five winters ago, a rider come to Belmont. Wasn't long 'fore Mas' Henley come to the kitchen with the news. "Rissa is dead," he said, his voice soundin' flat like unleavened bread. Didn't take long for the words to take hold. Mama was gone on to glory – just gone.

I remember hearin' the people in the Quarters singin' all through the night –

Crossin' over, crossin' over,
crossin' over into Zion.
Crossin' over, crossin' over,
the beautiful city of God.

When I finished my story, Spicy said, "Your story is my story." Then we both cried. After talkin' to Spicy I felt lots better. Spicy and I have laughed together, cried together and shared each other's hurts. We're becomin' good friends. I like that.

Monday

Mas' Henley and Hince have gone to a race over in Chester. Miz Lilly been into it with William all mornin'. He stormed out of the house and spent the mornin' with Uncle Heb at the stables. There was no lesson today.

Tuesday

Durin' study time, the Missus turned to figurin' numbers – and numbers don't come to me quick like the letters and words do. But even as bad as I am, William is still worse.

Wednesday, June 1, 1859

There was a meetin' at Belmont this evenin'. While I was servin' up sweets and coffee, I overheard Mas' Henley say he's supportin' a Cleophus Tucker who is runnin' for congress. Mas' Henley is plannin' to put on a big party in his honour on the 4th of July.

"Tucker's the man we need in Washington," Mas' Henley told members of the group.

They left a newspaper on the table, so when I was cleanin' up, I hid it under my dress to read later.

Next day

I read as much of the newspaper as I could, pickin' out words I know. It's still a heap of words I don't know. But I did find out abolistines are A-B-O-L-I-T-I-O-N-I-S-T-S. I know the right spellin' of the words now. I also found out that abolitionists live in places called the New York, the

Boston and the Philadelphia. Then there's somethin' called a underground railroad that slaves ride on to get away to freedom. I really want to know more 'bout that. I wrote all these names on a piece of paper. I'll bind my time. When the chance comes, I'll try to find these things on Mas' Henley's book of maps.

Friday

The rains have finally stopped. No rain all this week. Now the long heat sets in. Mosquitoes are busy, but we've burned rags almost every night to keep them away.

Saturday

Mas' Henley and Hince went to a horse race and Uncle Heb drove Miz Lilly and William to a neighbour lady's house for the day. So, that meant I could slip into Mas' Henley's study to see the map without gettin' caught. I found the same names I'd written down – the places where abolitionists live.

First, there was the Philadelphia, then the New York and the Boston. I found the Richmond and lots of other places I heared Uncle Heb and Hince talk 'bout. But that's all I can understand 'bout the map. All the lines stand for somethin' I know, but I don't know yet what they stand for. I wrote down as many names off that map as I could get on a sheet of paper, so when I write the names they will be spelled right. All these words got to do with freedom, so I'm hopin' all over myself that they will give me a picture of freedom.

Sunday

The river is high and the lowlands are flooded. Rufus talked about the Great Flood. Noah and his family went inside the ark and God, himself, locked the door. Noah and all the animals were safe inside the ark. Then the rain started fallin'. And the waters came a-gushin' up out of the ground and everythin' and everybody was drowned. All 'cept'n, Noah, his family and the animals.

Everybody say, Amen. I really didn't understand the story. I couldn't see in my mind the world all under water. It's like this. I read the words over William's shoulder sometimes, but I don't all the time get what the words mean.

Then Rufus told us his new little son was named Noah, 'cause God saved Noah from the drownin' waters. "God's gon' save us one day, too – but I'm talkin' 'bout bein' saved in the Biblistic way," he said. "Amen."

Monday

I just got one thing to ask – Why did God let mosquitoes get on the ark?

Sunday week – second Sunday in June

All week we worked and waited for Sunday. June heat feels hotter than the same heat in May. It was hard to sit still while Rufus told the story of David. When David was 'bout my age, he was a shepherd boy. He stood down a giant named Goliath with a slingshot and five smooth stones. "We must be like David," Rufus told us. "When we find ourselves facin' a giant, we must not run, but face the monster with the courage of David." Everybody said "Amen", even me. But, I didn't feel strong enough to beat up on a giant. Rufus tells good stories, but I just don't understand what makes them so great.

First thing afterwards, Missy come switchin' up to Hince grinnin'. I don't like Missy much any more – and I don't think it has a thing to do with Spicy. I just don't like the way she is.

Monday

It's June 17, 1859. I know 'cause I slipped ink out of Mas' Henley's study today – and a newspaper that was in the trash. Sometimes I surprise myself at the things I do just so I can keep learnin'.

Followin' Saturday

I am writin' by the light of a full moon. There was a lot of excitement today. Mas' Henley and Hince rode in from Fredericksburg. Been gone all week. They brought back a beautiful stallion named Dancer, a gift for William. "He's all yours," the mas'er told his son.

Everybody knew Mas' Henley was just showin' off. The horse was really a racehorse and Hince would be the one who would ride and care for it. But to keep Miz Lilly from fussin' 'bout turnin' Belmont into "a gamblin' den", Mas' Henley pretended he bought the horse for William.

It was so good to see Hince. As soon as he could get away from the stables, he came to the kitchen to speak. He was full of Dancer talk – went on and on 'bout how he was goin' to win a hundred races ridin' him.

Third Sunday in June

Uncle Heb left early this mornin', takin' the Missus to visit the Ambrose Plantation. They'll be gone all day. Rufus talked on Jonah. I liked that story, but I think it would be scary livin' in the belly of a big fish for three days and nights.

"We might find ourselves in the belly of a big fish at any time – but we must not be afraid. We must stay prayed up. Stay strong. Our faith will turn sour on the fish's stomach and it will have to deliver us – free us . . . Let us pray."

I got on to Rufus's Bible stories today. All the weeks he been leadin' us in service, he been tellin' us two stories in one. His stories are 'bout Bible times, but they is 'bout our times, too. Jonah in the belly of a big fish, Daniel and the lions and David and the giant is like us bein' in slavery, facin' the mas'ers. But God delivered Daniel, David and Jonah and he'll deliver us one day. Rufus can't say all that right out or Mas' Henley will make us stop havin' service. But Rufus tells us that in other ways. I didn't understand the stories at first, but now I do. For the first time, I said "Amen" and knew why I was sayin' it.

Monday

I went to the stables to visit Hince for a few minutes and to take a closer look at Dancer. The horse is every bit as fine as Hince said – not like any other. It would take a good rider like Hince to hold him steady though.

"A sure winner!" Hince say real proud-like.

"And he's mine," said William comin' through the door, dressed to ride. "Saddle him up."

William has been ridin' since he could straddle a horse. But anybody can see that Dancer is too much horse for him.

"William," said Hince, patient-like. "Dancer is not ready for you yet. Let me work with him a little 'fore you take him out."

The boy whined and fretted, but at last, he went on and rode Diamond. Still there was somethin' in the boy's voice that let us know he was bent, bound and sure to ride Dancer.

Last week in June

There won't be any more lessons until after the 4th of July holiday.

I hate holidays.

Every day there is somethin' for us to do. We're either cleanin' the house, fixin' the meals, servin' the meals, cleanin' up after the meals. No sooner than we're finished, it's time to start all over again.

When guests come, it's double work. We have to tote hot water for the guest's baths, empty the water after the baths and don't forget cleanin' chamber pots and makin' beds at first light in the mornin'. That's why I hate holidays.

Friday, July 1

Today Spicy and I were scrubbin' floors, gettin' ready for the 4th, but movin' like inch worms creepin' along. All of a sudden, Hince hopped up on the windowsill from the porch side. Almost scared us to death. "Okay, girls, why you movin' so slow? Get busy."

"When did we get a new mas'er?" Spicy said, bein' sassy.

"I'd be a poor mas'er to own the two of you," he said with that devilish look in his eyes. "Clotee, you aine big as a chickadee. So, I wouldn't sell you." He turned to Spicy. "And you there, gal, with the dark eyes. I wouldn't sell you either!" Then he added, "I'd just keep you for myself."

I could feel Spicy bein' happy, even though she held her head down.

"You like my brother-friend, don't you?" I asked Spicy when Hince was gone.

"He's not so bad," she say, and went back to scrubbin' the floors. This time she was a-movin' along faster, and hummin'.

July 2

Hince brought Spicy a handful of flowers this mornin'. He shoved them at her from the kitchen door. He aine never done nothin' like that 'fore. "For you," he said. 'Fore Spicy could answer, he ducked away and was gone. He missed seein' the big grin that lit up her whole face.

Aunt Tee just shook her head and poured some water in a cup and handed it to Spicy for the flowers. We both been teasin' her all day, 'bout bein' courted.

July 4

Sunday rest was cancelled for everybody. Too much work to do to get ready for the 4th.

I'm so tired. We got our regular work to do and some more – I don't know what day it was. I was up all night yesterday, workin' in the kitchen with Aunt Tee. Aggie and Wook came to help. Missy sees after the baby and helped

69

out, too, when he was asleep. I did all the fetchin' – runnin' from the springhouse to the smokehouse, to the Big House, to the house garden, to the barn and back. "Get me this" and "Get me that." I am writin' this late at night. Ready to crawl into a hole and sleep, but I cain't. Now its time to start cleanin' up.

July 6

Things are finally gettin' back to normal. It will take me days to write 'bout all that happened on the 4th.

Guests started comin' to Belmont early Monday mornin', campin' out on the grounds. Miz Lilly's daughter Clarissa and family were the first to arrive.

Clarissa's husband is Mr Richard Davies, a lawyer with a fine firm in the city. He's full of seriousness and she's a ball of nerves. I like her though. Maybe it's 'cause she's like a scared rabbit, 'bout ready to run for cover. Not at all like her mama. I can't say much for Miz Clarissa's two sons. Richard Jr and Wilbur, who are close to the same age as William, keep somethin' goin' all the time. When William gets with them, they spell T-R-O-U-B-L-E. Trouble.

Soon as Richard and Wilbur set first foot out of the

carriage, William came tearin' out of the house like it was on fire. Then all three of them began runnin' through the house, screamin' and yellin', out the back door, leapin' over the hedges, trampin' in the flower beds. Their mama just looked on like it's as natural as the risin' sun. Nobody 'spects better of 'em, so they act that way.

By mid-mornin' on the 4th, many more guests had come. Mas' Henley tried to be real gentleman-like, greetin' people, welcomin' them, shakin' hands. But no matter how much he tries to look the part of a real gentleman, he's still seen as a gambler who got lucky enough to marry a woman with money.

Miz Lilly, on the other hand, was like a fly, flutterin' 'bout in that ugly green dress. She was lightin' just long enough to say a few words then off to another guest. At times like these it's hard to see her slappin' us or yellin' at us 'til the veins in her neck bulge out like she'd been doin' all mornin'. My face is still stingin' where she slapped me for walkin' too slow. Walkin' too slow. I was so tired I was glad to be walkin' at all.

Everybody ate like dogs, gobblin' up pots of smoked ham and beans, fresh greens, smothered chicken, gravy and rice, and all kinds of pies and cakes. Nobody ever thought 'bout how hard we'd all had to work to fix it. They just ate.

On full stomachs, Mas' Henley didn't have no more sense than to call everybody together to hear Cleophus Tucker, the man who Mas' Henley wanted people to vote for. Mr Tucker's talk was full of too many words, but people were nice 'bout pretendin' to listen. I was half asleep, until I heard the word abolitionist, then I listened real close.

"I, for one, am tired of abolitionists tellin' me what I should do with my slaves. I'm tired of lawless meddlers comin' into our communities and spiritin' away our nigras on this so-called Underground Railroad."

It felt good to know these words, but I still didn't get a full understandin' of what they meant.

July 7

Pickin' up from yesterday. . .

Hince was set to ride Dancer against a horse named Wind Away, brought up from Atlanta, that was supposed to be the fastest horse on four feet. Just 'bout everybody bet on the Atlanta mount.

I overheard Mas' Henley whisper to Hince, "You'd better ride him to win, boy, or else." Hince laughed in a devil-may-care way and spurred Dancer onto the field.

"Come on, Hince," I shouted, knowin' that if he lost, he'd have Mas' Henley to reckon with. All the folks from the Quarters was pullin' for him to win, includin' Missy. Aunt Tee screamed so, she plum lost her voice. But it was Spicy – Spicy who out-shouted us all! I wasn't the only one to notice it either. I caught Missy givin' Spicy a mean, mean look.

Hince didn't need our cheerin', 'cause he won with room to spare. Mas' Henley carried on so, braggin' and all, folks started findin' excuses to leave.

In the far away I just heard the sound of a train. I wonder is it on the Underground Railroad. I could see in my head slaves on the train headin' for the Philadelphia, the New York and the Boston. The picture made me smile. One day I want to ride that train.

July 10

Clarissa and the boys have been here since the 4th. They go home today. Nobody will be unhappy to see the backs of their heads. While I served breakfast to William and his nephews, I heard William talkin' 'bout ridin' Dancer by himself. "When you ride up in front of our house in Richmond, then we'll believe he's your horse," said Richard.

I hope William is not goin' to be silly enough to ride Dancer that far by himself. Should I tell Miz Lilly, so maybe she'll speak to him 'bout it?

Second Monday in July

All of the guests are gone home now. We spent the mornin' straightenin' up the guest rooms. It's sick hot, but no matter, I have to weed the house garden. The hat Hince gave me really helps. I hardly ever take it off.

Somethin' was eatin' up my tomato vines. Uncle Heb say put tobacco juice on the leaves. I'd seen him use it before on his roses. So I bit off a piece of tobacco and chewed it to make the juice. Lord, I swallowed some. My head started swimmin' and my stomeck heaved up everythin' I had eaten for breakfast – two days ago.

I've never been so sick in my whole life. Thought for a minute, I was dyin'. How can anybody chew tobacco? I won't ever again. The worms can have the tomatoes.

Tuesday

I saw William down at the stables. He was talkin' to some of the hands. I thought maybe I should tell Miz Lilly what I overheared.

"I think he may try to ride Dancer over to Richmond," I told her.

"Don't be foolish, Clotee. William wouldn't try to do a dangerous thing like that." She made me brush her hair before she sent me away. Maybe she's right. But somehow I don't think so.

Early Thursday mornin'

We polished silver all day. Miz Lilly went over every tray, pitcher, bowl and candlestick. She found one little spot on a silver tray that I had cleaned and she slapped me so hard I saw stars. I don't get hit often, but when I do, I try to be like Spicy and not let her see me cry. "Spicy is bein' a bad inflewance on you," she said, and slapped Spicy, too. Miz Lilly is awful 'cause she know we cain't hit her back. If one of us whacked her back across her face, I bet she wouldn't be so quick to hit. I got to be careful not to put ideas like hittin' the Missus in my head. Aunt Tee say if you think 'bout hittin' back, you'll soon strike-out, hit back. And to fight a missus or a mas'er means death for sure.

Next evenin'

Durin' dinner, Spicy and I served hot bread and poured water for the Henleys. We came in on Mas' Henley and Miz Lilly fussin' 'bout William gettin' somethin' called a tooter. When Mas' Henley said no, Miz Lilly would not let it be.

As the word-fight 'tween them heated up, Spicy took off the soup bowls and I served the fried chicken. Miz Lilly won that battle.

Later, the three of us – Spicy, Aunt Tee and me had our supper together. Whenever Aunt Tee fries chicken for the Henleys, she fries the chicken neck, gizzard, liver and the-last-part that goes over the fence, and makes a thick brown gravy for us. Eat that with some biscuits and honey – good eatin'.

Spicy and me had Aunt Tee bent over laughin,' pokin' fun

at Miz Lilly's faked faintin' spells. Spicy did a perfect Miz Lilly swoon. "Ohhhh, he'll be the first Monroe not to get into Overton School!"

I played the Mas'er. "My mind is made up – William will not have a tooter." Then I belched and raised up a hip and pretended to pass gas.

"You girls is a mess," Aunt Tee say, hangin' up the dish towel and blowin' out the kitchen candles. I stretched out on my straw-filled pallet next to Spicy.

"Anybody know what a tooter is?" I had been waitin' for the right moment to ask. Nobody knew. I'll add it to my list of words. I figured it had somethin' to do with William's schoolin'. Wonder will it mean I cain't get no more learnin'?

Day later

Spicy and I spent the evenin' workin' in the house garden with Uncle Heb. We helped him tie strips of old rags on a measure of line to shoo the critters away. He told us stories 'bout a spider-man that could talk. Uncle Heb say his mama told him these old spider stories. He say his mama come from Afric. Say white men fell upon them one day and threw nets over her and some other girls. Then they put them on a boat and brought them 'cross the big water. Say that's how all our peoples got here. We come here from Afric on white men's boats.

I once heared Aunt Tee talk 'bout the Afric woman named Belle who taught her 'bout root doctorin' and birthin'. I aine never seen nobody that was natural-born Afric. I'd like to though.

Monday, July 18, 1859

I found out what a tooter is. It is a tutor. Miz Lilly wrote it for William. He's a teacher. Heared Miz Lilly tellin' William durin' lesson that his name is Ely Harms. And he's comin' here in August. He's comin' from a place called Washington, D.C. I know from lessons that's where the President of the land lives in a big white house. Reckon does this Mr Harms know the President?

Miz Lilly say the tutor will stay here on the place and his only job will be to teach William. I hope I'll get to fan them durin' their lessons, so I can go on learnin'.

Wednesday

The Missus has had Spicy and me busy for the past few days cleanin' her own personal room. We stayed busy for hours, scrubbin' the floors, beatin' rugs, airin' mattresses and re-stuffin' pillows.

At the end of the day, Missus called me to her side. "You know that your mama and I were the best of friends?" she said. "You're smart, just like her."

"Why'd you let her go?" I don't know what come over me. Aunt Tee is right. If you think on a thing, you'll end up doin' it. How many times had I thought about askin' her that question? Now I'd dared to ask it. The words just popped right out of my mouth. It's a wonder she didn't slap me. Instead she just gave me a warnin'. "Must not be sassy, Clotee." Then she studied my face. I was sure my eyes had turned into windows and she could see all the letters and words tumblin' 'round in my brain. So I closed my eyes, too scared to move.

"Yes. You're different from the others. I never know quite what's goin' on inside that little head of yours. But it makes me wonder."

Miz Lilly is scary like a bad dream.

Later

Come to find out, Miz Lilly promised to give Spicy the same white handkerchief with purple and yellow pansies on each corner if she brought her things 'bout me.

"I'm not a tattler," she said. "Besides that's the ugliest handkerchief I ever seen!"

So Miz Lilly is lookin' for somethin' on me, now. I trust Spicy not to tell. But who else has she tempted? I got to be so careful. I just wrote D-A-N-G-E-R. I see Miz Lilly's face.

Thursday

At least I'm learnin' from Miz Lilly. I learned today that there's no such word as knowed. It's knew. I never knew that. I do now.

Fourth Saturday in July

Somethin' awful done happened. I knew it. Knew it. William has left here, ridin' Dancer over to Richmond – showin' off.

It started when Hince and Mas' Henley were gone 'way to a race. William went to Uncle Heb, sayin' his daddy had said he could ride Dancer. I told Miz Lilly he'd do it, but she didn't b'lieve me. So, Uncle Heb saddled up Dancer. Last we seen of the boy, he shot out of the stables and down the drive. I got a real bad feelin' aine nothin' good comin' out of this for nobody.

Early the next mornin'

Miz Lilly sent Rufus and other riders out to follow William, but couldn't no horse in the county catch Dancer. All we could do was wait. Not long, the horse came trottin' back up the drive, draggin' William's body like a sack of rags. It was clear the boy had fallen off, but his foot had gotten caught.

Everythin' that happened next is a blur. Somebody went to fetch Dr Lamb – but it took over two hours for him to get to Belmont. Meanwhile, Aunt Tee did everything she could to help. Spicy and I stood in the shadows of William's room, ready to fetch and hold whatever the doctor needed.

I heard Miz Lilly ask, "Will he live?" I prayed that William would live. I hope God will forgive my selfish reason. I prayed William would live 'cause I knew Mas' Henley would make our lives miserable if his son died.

"Oh, yes," the doctor said, pattin' Miz Lilly on her arm. "He'll live. William's a tough little character." I felt better. Miz Lilly's shoulders relaxed, too. She looked at me and for a second I looked straight into her eyes. I dropped my eyes quickly, 'cause we aine s'posed to look Mas'er and Missus in the eye. But for that quick second I seen somethin'. I seen that she knew that I knew that I had warned her 'bout this, and she had not listened. She was thinkin' 'bout it, too.

"But," added Dr Lamb. We all listened to what was comin' next. Sadness clouded the doctor's face. "I'm not so sure William will ever walk again."

Miz Lilly really did faint. All I can think 'bout is that it's gon' be awful when Mas' Henley gets home.

Day later – Monday, July 25, 1859

When Mas' Henley heared 'bout William, he went straight 'way to the barn and shot Dancer, a single bullet in the horse's head – like that was gon' make William well again. We could hear Hince cryin' over that horse most of the night.

Then Mas'er come lookin' for Uncle Heb – got it in his head that Uncle Heb was to blame for what happened to William, so he came to kill him – just like the horse. Me and Spicy done learned that in times like these it is best to stay out of the way. We watched everythin' from the room over the kitchen – holdin' one another, tremblin', tryin' not to cry out.

Po' Uncle Heb tried to say what happened, but Mas' Henley went to beatin' him with the barrel of the gun – beatin' him all in the head. I heard the licks – hard licks over Aunt Tee's screamin'. Uncle Heb fell down, and Mas' Henley kicked him and pointed the gun at the ol' man's head.

"Don't kill him, please," Aunt Tee begged for her husband's life. For some reason he didn't pull the trigger. He might as well have though, 'cause Uncle Heb died in Aunt Tee's arms an hour or so later. His big heart just stopped.

Later

Mas' Henley come to the kitchen to see Aunt Tee when they told him 'bout Uncle Heb dyin' and all. He come sayin', "I lost my temper a bit. I wasn't really goin' to kill the old man. You've got to believe that."

When Aunt Tee didn't say nothin', he raised his voice in an angry way. "My boy is up there, unable to walk 'cause that old man let him ride Dancer. He's to blame. He should have known better."

Blame? Mas' Henley don't care nothin' 'bout the real truth. He just make the truth what he wants it to be. The truth is, Mas' was the one who brung Dancer to Belmont and gave him to William. Mas'ers can do that. But Mas' Henley will never make me b'lieve what I know aine so.

"Now, you listen to me," he say, pointin' his finger in Aunt Tee's face. "I don't want you holdin' what happened to Uncle Heb against me, you hear? That old man just died. I didn't kill him."

Aunt Tee looked at her master long and hard – like she was lookin' at him for the first time. "You aine got to worry, I won't poison you. I aine that low-down and ornery."

Rufus tells us to hate the sin and not the sinner. I hate slavery so bad, it's mighty hard sometimes not to hate the slave masters – men like Mas' Henley.

Sunrise Tuesday

We held Uncle Heb's funeral this mornin' when it was mornin' but not yet day. 'Fore we had to go to the fields and to the kitchen, we stopped to say farewell to Uncle Heb. He was like a lovin' grandfather to me.

Women from the Quarters came last night and helped Aunt Tee get Uncle Heb's body ready for burial. The men folk went to the cemetery to dig the grave. All the folks from the Quarters came and we sat and sang and prayed. Rufus talked 'bout the peace of death – no more sufferin' – no more pain. I fanned Uncle Heb's body, keepin' the flies away – up and down, up and down. Then I dared to touch him. I'd never touched a dead person 'fore and I knew it would be scary, but it wasn't. Po' Uncle Heb. He felt hard and cold. Not like him. The him that used to be Uncle Heb had flew up to heaven.

At the time when Aunt Tee say she was ready, we wrapped him in a clean white sheet and put him in a cart and carried him to the plantation cemetery where all Miz Lilly's people are buried – her father and mother and grandfather. Miz Lilly came – had nerve enough to cry. Mas' Henley didn't even bother to show up. How could anybody think we were lucky livin' close to people like them?

One sweet song –

Still by the river
waitin' for my Saviour
to come for me.
Goin' home, goin' home
to be with God.

Rufus spoke kindly over Uncle Heb, sayin' how good he was and how he had lived. I could feel the hot tears behind my eyes, thinkin' all the while that Uncle Heb would still be alive if Mas' Henley hadn't killed him.

Aunt Tee just looked off into space – thinkin' her own thoughts – never once cryin'. She had cried dry. Hince took it real hard. Uncle Heb had been like a grandfather to him, too – all of us, really. Spicy did what she could to comfort us, even though she had her own sorrow to bear.

Everybody kept sayin' Uncle Heb was free at last. Why do we have to die to be free? Why can't we be free and live?

Wednesday

For the first time as long as I can remember, Aunt Tee didn't fix fried chicken and whipped potatoes today. I wasn't the onlyest person to notice it, either.

Thursday

I've been tryin' to piece together all that's done went on for the last few days. No time to grieve, 'cause our work aine never stopped. Mas' Henley wants his food served on time and the Missus wants her house cleaned, her bed made, her water brought up for baths and on and on and on – no end to the work she thinks up for us to do.

Aunt Tee misses Uncle Heb so much, she just shakes with hurt. Then she sings a lot –

Help me, help me, help me, Jesus.
Help me, help me, help me, Lord.

Father, you know that I'm not able
To climb this mountain by myself.
Help me, help me, help me, Jesus.
Help me, help me, help me, Lord.

Nobody should have to live as a slave. If a slave can be an abolitionist, then I want to be one, 'cause I hate slavery and I want it to end.

Friday

Whenever I write the word F-L-O-W-E-R I will think of that kindly old man who grew beautiful roses and told the best stories ever.

After the dinner meal, Spicy and I walked through Uncle Heb's flower beds all the way down to the river. The sunflowers were turned toward the evenin' sun. I remembered Uncle Heb called me his little Sunflower Girl. He said my face always looked like it was facin' the sun – full of brightness. I squeezed Little Bit, my birthday doll, which I've come to carryin' 'round in my apron pocket. I like the feel of the smooth wood on my hand. That would please Uncle Heb. My thoughts made me smile. Spicy found a four-leafed clover. It's s'posed to bring good luck. We sure could use some 'round this place.

Saturday

Spicy and me took Miz Lilly's bath water up to her room. She sent Spicy out, but she asked me to stay and fan her for a while. I obeyed.

"Clotee, things are goin' to change 'round here. But, I'm takin' care of you. Don't you worry. Just promise me you won't say a word 'bout your talk with me 'bout William. I never dreamed that he would do somethin' so stupid. STUPID!"

I think Miz Lilly is worried that if Mas' Henley finds out I had warned her 'bout William's plan to ride Dancer and she'd done nothin' to stop him, he would be really, really mad with her. Now she's tryin' to still my mouth with favours. What is gettin' ready to change 'round here? And how is Miz Lilly gon' help me? None of this makes me feel very good in the stomeck.

Two weeks later

I saw the calendar in Mas' Henley's office. We in August already. August 10, 1859. So much has happened since last I wrote in my diary. I knew somethin' was comin', but didn't know what. Mas' Henley done changed everythin' – everythin'. Nothin's the same.

First, he moved Aunt Tee out of the kitchen. Say he cain't trust her to cook for him no more, 'cause of what happened to Uncle Heb. He put her down in the Quarters to look after the babies. Then to make it worse, he done brung Eva Mae up to the kitchen to be his new cook.

There's more. Missy is takin' Spicy's place, 'cause Spicy's been sent to the fields. I get to stay in the kitchen, doin' what I been doin'. I guess that's what Miz Lilly meant when she say she was gon' take care of me. I'd just as soon go to the Quarters with Aunt Tee than to stay near Miz Lilly.

Spicy aine sorry to be goin' to the fields. She say she'll miss talkin' to me all hours of the night. I will miss spendin' hours talkin' to her under the stars. I will miss her stumblin' and fallin', then laughin' 'bout it. Things will not be the same up here in the Big House without her.

Aunt Tee is who I worry 'bout. This is the thanks she gets after all those years of service. Mas'ers don't care how long and hard we work for them. They own us, so they can do whatever they want to us. That's the worse part of bein' a slave. Never havin' a say in what happens to yourself.

Third Monday in August

Everybody knows that Eva Mae aine half the cook Aunt Tee is. But she likes to think that she is.

It hurt me when Miz Lilly wouldn't let Aunt Tee take the old iron bed she and Uncle Heb had slept in for years. The bed had been a gift from Miz Lilly's grandfather to Uncle Heb for his years of service. Now Miz Lilly done gave it to Eva Mae and Missy to sleep in. It's not right that Aunt Tee should have to sleep on a pallet at her age. When we abolitionists end slavery, everybody will have a bed to sleep in. Wonder will I ever get to meet a real abolitionist?

Next day

A horse and buggy turned into the front gate, gallopin' at full speed. Whenever I write the word S-T-R-A-N-G-E, I will remember seein' Mr Ely Harms bouncin' 'round in that buggy, comin' up the drive. The tutor is here and I can't wait to find out 'bout him.

Monday again

The tutor's been here a week. He's a little freckled-faced man with a shock of red hair that sticks out of the side of his hat. He looks like he's been pieced together from parts took from other folks. His teeth got a big gap in the middle and his legs and arms seem a bit too long and too thin for the rest of hisself. I can't guess his years, but he's got young eyes that look at you over cloudy glasses that sits on the tip of his nose. I'll guess and give him 'bout 25 years – give or take one or two.

Miz Lilly fluttered on and on 'bout how sorry she was that nobody – nobody – had told Mr Harms not to come 'cause of William's bad fall. Mr Harms used a lot of fast words – real fancy-like. And by the end of supper, he had Mas' Henley and Miz Lilly set on him stayin' on here at Belmont.

I was glad, 'cause if William's studies stop, then so would mine. Trouble is, what sort of tutor was Mr Harms gon' be?

After the dinner meal that same day

Things in the kitchen be a big mess! Eva Mae got her own way of doin', her own recipes. When I try to show her somethin' she tells me to shut up. "I'm the mistress of the kitchen, now." So, I decided to just let her alone – do what I'm s'posed to do and keep my mouth shut – just like she say.

Week later

Dr Lamb came by – say William was well enough to start studyin' – an hour or so a day, and added it would be good for the boy. The first lesson time with Mr Harms was today in William's bedroom. I was standin' in my place ready to fan.

"Why are you here?" Mr Harms asked, lookin' at me over the top of his glasses.

William s'plained that I was a fanner. Mr Harms say they didn't need a fanner. My heart sunk down to my toes. My learnin' would have ended right then, too, if William hadn't gone to whinin' 'bout how it was too hot. He let me stay. I never thought I'd be glad to hear William's whinin'.

Few days later

I went down to Aunt Tee's cabin in the Quarters after the last meal. That gave me a chance to visit with her and Spicy. She's holdin' her own, but it's got to be hard on Aunt Tee, losin' first Uncle Heb and then her job.

They live in a real small cabin now with a dirt floor – no windows, only a door that don't shut all the way. Yet, everybody in the Quarters is seein' after Aunt Tee. All them years Aunt Tee took care of them and they children, now they payin' her back with love and kindness. Aine none of them got much, but what they got, they's willin' to share.

I slipped out a piece or two of day-old bread and a few

leftovers for her to fill out their meal. I told them how Missy and Eva Mae had changed. They are thick with Miz Lilly, grinnin' and smilin', gettin' in with her. Before I left, I told Aunt Tee 'bout my warnin' Miz Lilly 'bout William and her not listenin'. "She's scared I'll tell Mas' Henley." Aunt Tee agreed. She took me to her heart. "Be careful, chile. Miz Lilly aine gon' stand for you to have nothin' over her head. She'll keep on 'til she find somethin' on you to use – to get rid of you – to keep you down. She'll use them two in the kitchen to help her. To win favours, Eva Mae and Missy will tell everythin' they know and then make up some. Be particular, and watch as well as pray."

Now I've got to be very, very careful 'bout my readin' and writin', 'cause now Miz Lilly is lookin' for somethin'. Now I know how Daniel must have felt in the lion's den.

Thursday night

Woke up after dreamin' 'bout Mama – all in a sweat. It was unlike any dream I've ever had 'bout her. She was standin' beside Mr Harms. He was smilin' at me, all the while Mama was sayin', "It's gon' be jus' fine, baby girl. It's gon' be jus' fine."

Rufus say, God talks to us in dreams. If that's so, then I wonder what God is tryin' to tell me?

Last Monday in August

Calendar say it's August 29, 1859.

Mr Harms brought a book to study time. William wouldn't read it. Mr Harms never said a word. He opened the book and he started to read. "Long ago, in a far away place called Greze there lived a great hero named Herquelez."

I knew Mas'er John Hamby's slave named Herquelez who lived on a nearby plantation. He was powerful strong, too. But this was not a story 'bout him.

Mr Harms told us how the long-ago Herquelez killed a big serpent. Then the teacher-man stopped, closed the book and walked away without sayin' another word.

"There's more, right?" William called out.

"Tomorrow," said Mr Harms.

I can't wait to find out more, too.

First day of September

There was a big race up in Winchester last week, and Hince won. Soon as he got back, he came to the kitchen to see me and to tell me all 'bout his win. First thing, Missy come sidin' up to him – like he came there to see her. He asked where Spicy was, right in front of her. I gladly told him.

Monday

Mr Harms starts each day by sayin' the day, month and year. Today is Monday, September 5, 1859. So, now I can keep better track of time.

Tuesday, September 6, 1859

William has taken to Mr Harms like a bird to berries. I declare, the boy is reading now and liking it. I'm learning a lot, too. I'm adding "ing" to my words now, 'cause Mr Harms made William stop saying, "talkin'", and "walkin'" and "singin'". It is talking, walking and singing. I remember to write my ings, but I still forget to say my ings.

Wednesday, September 7, 1859

Mr Harms has taken charge of William's days. Two men from down in the Quarters comes up every morning and helps William get bathed and dressed. One brings William down for breakfast in his rolling chair. Afterwards, we have our study time – in the cool of the morning – just hot enough to need a fanner, which is still me. Then it's time for lunch. William eats with Mr Harms most of the time. The rest of the day William listens to Mr Harms read to him, or they play card games, or a game called chess. William spends the evenin' with his mother and father – but most time they spat 'bout one thing or another, so he goes off to bed.

Thursday, September 8, 1859

I slipped out late last night. Came out to write in my diary. I heard a twig snap. Someone was coming. I called to see who it was. Missy answered, asking, "What you doing out here?"

I was sitting on my diary. I told her it was too hot to sleep, so I'd come out to look at the stars.

"Why do you always come back here behind the kitchen?"

She was digging for a bone. "I like it back here. I can see the river and the stars."

My hiding place behind the kitchen is no longer safe. I have to find a new place, safer, and real soon.

Friday, September 9, 1859

Since Uncle Heb's been dead, the garden's been looking real pitiful. I pulled a few weeds from 'round the roses. But it just aine the same. I miss him and sometimes turn 'round to say something to him, but he's not there. He never will be there, just like Mama.

Oh, yes, I learned from Mr Harms that it's around and not 'round. It's something and not somethin'. I've got more out of Mr Harms' lesson than I ever did from Miz Lilly.

But there's something real different about Mr Harms, and I cain't put it to words yet. He never even looks at me. Treats me like I'm not there.

Saturday, September 10, 1859

I was digging through some of the trash in Mas' Henley's study, looking for things about abolitionists and the Underground Railroad. Nothing. I cain't find a thing to help me understand my list of words better. So, when I just wrote F-R-E-E-D-O-M, it still don't show me no picture. But I'm keeping my eyes open.

Sunday, September 11, 1859

Aunt Tee been so sad since she been turned out of the kitchen. I would do anything to help make her laugh and be happy again. I guess that's why I did a very foolish thing. I went down to her cabin to visit. After we'd talked, I used a stick to scratch writing on the dirt floor. C is for CAT.

Before I could blink my eye, Aunt Tee had slapped me so hard I had to hold on to the table to keep from toppling over. Miz Lilly aine never hit me that hard. She rubbed out the letters with her foot. At last, my head stopped swimming and the spots before my eyes cleared up. There wasn't no anger in Aunt Tee's eyes, only fear.

"Do you know what happen to slaves the mas'er finds out got learnin'?" she whispered sternly.

I knew they got beaten, or much worse they got sold to the Deep South. I couldn't make her understand that I was trusting her. I knew she wouldn't tell on me.

"I don't wanna be trusted," Aunt Tee say, near tears.

"Look at what trust got me. I b'lieved Mas' Henley would do right by me, 'cause I'd done right by him. Not so. Look at me now. Trusting got me here. Who teached you, chile?"

I was scared to say – and real sorry I'd told her about any of it. I decided to hold back on all the truth. "I teached myself just a few words."

Aunt Tee sucked in her breath and clicked her teeth. Her face was clouded over with worry. "Don't bring trouble to yo' own front door," she say, biting her lip, the way she did when she was real worried. "Don't you tell another living soul that you got this little piece of knowing. You hear me?"

Never have I been more sure of anything. I will not tell another person my secret ever.

After study time – Monday, September 12, 1859

Now Mr Harms is on to something! And I brought the trouble to my own front door.

He and William was reading a play together. As usual I was standing behind them, fanning – up and down, up and down – and reading over their shoulders. William got stuck on the word "circumstances". I was so taken by the story, I plum forgot where I was. Suddenly, my mouth got ahead of my thoughts and I blurted out the first part of the word. "Cir—" I caught myself, but not soon enough.

Mr Harms jerked around and looked at me – his mouth dropped open a little, like he was surprised. "What did you say?"

"Cir – yes, sir? Yes. Sir is what I said. Sir. Sir? May I go, please?" I was thinking fast – Lord let me get out of this.

Mr Harms looked down at the book, then he looked back up at me and where I was standing. He told me I could go, but asked my name. He knows – he knows! Lord! Lord! What's going to happen to me?

Wednesday, September 14, 1859

I guess I was wrong about Mr Harms being on to me. He aine said a thing, and I'm still fanning during lessons. I let up writing for a few days, 'cause I've been too scared to go near the hiding spot, what with Missy slipping around, and maybe Mr Harms is on to something.

Thursday, September 15, 1859

Spicy looks tired when she comes in from the fields. But she says the tobacco don't slap you in the face, and call you all hours of the night, and send you to do this or that. Spicy likes the fields better than working in the Big House.

Missy likes the Big House. She's struck by all the sparkle and pretty of the Mas'er's house. She go around touching things and oohing and aahing over it all. She so busy looking at stuff, she gets careless. I have to redo some of her work sometimes to keep us both out of trouble.

When I show her where she's made a mistake, Missy gets mad and starts yelling at me all hateful. "You just think you cute. Make me sick – all the time trying to talk all proper-like. You're just a skinny, little thing, so don't come trying to say I'm stupid." I never say she's stupid, even though I think it. And I don't try to talk proper-like.

Then before the evening is over good, she's back trying to be friends with me again. She always asking me a lot of questions about Hince. I know how to get back at Missy, though. I say, "Why don't you ask Spicy." It's hard to b'lieve we was ever friends. Missy bears watching.

Monday, September 19, 1859

Apple harvest time is almost over. The tall men been knocking apples and then we gathered them. I got to sort with the grown women this year – putting the big, the middle and the little apples in barrels. It aine the work I like – but I love to hear the women telling stories, remembering. I really like it when they tell a story 'bout my mama.

Tuesday, September 20, 1859

I've found a good hiding place for my diary in the hollow of a tree, just beyond the orchard. I feel safer coming here. My hiding place behind the kitchen was getting too dangerous. I sure miss the way things used to be when Uncle Heb was alive and Aunt Tee ran the kitchen. They were far less troublesome times than these are now.

Later the same day

After the last meal, Missy said to me all syrupy sweet, "We been friends for a long, long time, but I don't know you."

What was that supposed to mean? She knew me, sure.

"I know your name," she say, "and that you favour cornbread over biscuits. You'll take red colour over green colour, and you like being off by yourself. But I don't know you, Clotee. Like what makes you happy or what makes you cry? You're not like the others. You're different. What makes you different?"

I'd heard those words before. Miz Lilly had told me I was different, and she'd sent Missy digging for a bone.

"Friends share secrets," she say all friendly and nice. "Do you have one you want to share with me?"

"No," I said and got away from her as fast as I could. Missy is a tattler, sent straight from Miz Lilly. I know it.

Wednesday, September 21, 1859

I wish I could read Mr Harms as easy as I can read Missy and Eva Mae. There's something 'bout Mr Harms that sets me to wondering. He looks perculiar and he acts perculiar, so people don't pay close attention to him. They don't see him all the time watching, taking in everything that's being said and done. But I do.

Just a minute ago, I saw Mr Harms standing at the edge of the orchard, looking toward the woods and beyond the river. Just looking. Made me nervous – my diary being just a few feet from where he was standing. Maybe I need to move it again.

Aunt Tee and I have not spoke about my learning since I told her. Spicy put in that she'd seen Mr Harms watching them working in the fields. Just looking, saying nothing, just watching them work.

Monday, September 26, 1859

I brought my pallet to sleep outside. The stars are so bright,
I can almost hear them tinkling. But tonight I heard Rufus
singing – his beautiful voice riding on the night wind.

> *Steal away*
> *Steal away*
> *Steal away home. . .*

Was that Mr Harms I just seen heading for the Quarters? I
wonder who he be visiting this hour of the night? Oh well,
white men sometimes visit the Quarters in the dark of night,
when their wives and mothers aine watching. I'm surprised.
Mr Harms don't 'pear to be that kind of man.

Tuesday, September 27, 1859

Miz Lilly left this morning to visit her daughter Clarissa in Richmond. She goes every September. She'll be gone for several good weeks. These are always happy days for us who work in the Big House.

She usually takes William. And she'd promised to take me this year. But William flat wouldn't go this time. And for some reason, she took Missy instead. Good. I'll get a rest from the both of them. I'm staying with Spicy and Aunt Tee the whole time, even though Eva Mae promises to tell when Miz Lilly gets back.

Friday, September 30, 1859

Miz Lilly's gon'. Mas'er went sporting – will be gone until Monday. William is home, but he's in his room sleeping. Mr Harms is asleep, too. Belmont is a big play house when everybody's gone.

Spicy and me slipped up to Miz Lilly's bedroom. We put on her jewellery and scarves and hats. We sat at her desk where there is all kinds of pretty paper, and pens and ink a-plenty. I took enough to last me a good while.

We heard a noise outside in the yard. At first I thought it might be one of the dogs or a raccoon. We quick-like jumped out of the bed and ran to the window.

We seen Rufus come slipping from tree to tree then turn toward the Quarters. We figured he'd been out possum hunting. But, a little later, I seen Mr Harms creeping out from the other side of the woods. We watched as he stole from shadow to shadow until he reached the house and stepped inside. We held our breath until we heard his footsteps pass the door and go down the hall to his room.

We quietly cleaned up, put everything in its place and left Miz Lilly's bedroom just the way we found it.

What were Mr Harms and Rufus doing out in the woods together so late at night?

Monday, October 3, 1859

I've been staying with Aunt Tee down in the Quarters. She takes care of Baby Noah and the other children that cain't work yet. When Wook came to get the baby, we got a chance to visit. She aine seen her husband but twice since they got married. Seems he loved another girl from his own plantation and wanted to marry her. Wook has changed a lot. She looks so sad all the time.

I told her how Missy was acting, and she said she wasn't surprised. "Missy has always been for Missy – selfish." When we was growing up, I never knew that side of her, but Wook did. "If I got something, she wanted it, no matter how small it was. She's put out at me 'cause I got married first. She coulda got married ahead of me and I wouldn't a-cared at all."

Later, it was like old times in Aunt Tee's cabin. We sang, told stories and Spicy and me even got to work on our quilt.

Tuesday, October 4, 1859

Mr Harms fussed at William about saying 'cause instead of because. I learned it, too.

Later I took Hince his meal down at the stables. We talked for a good while. Him and me talking is fun. The words just pop right out of my head without me thinking on them long. "You ever think of running away?"

He studied on that for a spell. "Sometimes."

"What would you do if you was free?"

"I figures, if I be a free man, I could hire myself out as a jockey. I'd bet on myself and win and win and win, 'til I had 'nuf money to buy all of y'als freedom – Spicy, Aunt Tee, you, Clotee. That's what I would do."

When nobody was looking I wrote F-R-E-E-D-O-M in flour. It still don't show me no picture.

Later the same day

True to her word, Eva Mae told Mas' Henley that I'd been staying in the Quarters with Aunt Tee instead of in the kitchen. He spoke to me about it when we served him the last meal.

"Aunt Tee is like my mama," I said. "I'd like to stay with her."

"You want to stay down in the Quarters with Aunt Tee? Well, what does your mistress say about this?"

"I haven't asked her."

"When she comes home, ask her. See what she says. I'll go along with what she says. You're one of her favourites."

Me? I never thought of myself as being favoured by Miz Lilly, unless she wanted something from me.

Wednesday, October 5, 1859

Mas' Henley pitched a red-in-the-face fit 'bout Eva Mae's fried chicken. He called it tasteless slop! Serves him right.

Thursday, October 6, 1859

Tonight Spicy took me by the hand and led me to a hollowed out tree. My heart sank when I realized that it was the tree where my diary was hid. Had she found my diary? All of a sudden, Spicy blurted out that she had a book. To prove it, she reached in and pulled out a Bible. My diary was just inches away. "I've wanted to tell you this forever, but I been scared," she said.

Spicy had a Bible that had been her mama's. "My mama could read and write," said Spicy. Then she told me her mama's story. It was like others I'd heard. Spicy's mama tried to run away, but each time she got caught and beat bad. Finally her mas'er say if she ran away she was gon' get sold. Spicy's mama learned how to write – took her a while. Spicy was borned and still she kept learning. Then one day, she wrote herself a pass and tried to run again. But a slave who worked in the Big House told the mistress and she got caught. Before they sent Spicy's mama to the Deep South, she slipped Spicy the Bible.

"I done kept it all these years," Spicy said. "I cain't read a word that's in it, not yet. One day I will. But even if I don't ever read, I'll keep this Bible forever. It is all I have that b'longed to my mama."

Spicy hugged the book to her chest. "Nobody in the world knows about this book 'cept'n you. And I trust you won't tell, 'cause we're good friends."

Should I share my secret with Spicy? Good sense tells me that I shouldn't. But I want to so, so bad.

Monday, October 10, 1859

Mr Harms came storming into the kitchen, sputtering and making a grand fuss. He made Eva Mae and me stop what we was doing and listen to him.

"This has come to my attention," he said, holding up Spicy's Bible. "If it belongs to one of you, I want to know, now!" His eyes moved from face to face. "Speak," he shouted.

He could have saved his breath. Neither one of us owned it.

"I'm going to report this to Miz Lilly when she returns," he said.

"Yes, Mas' Harms," said Eva Mae.

The tutor tucked Spicy's Bible under his arm. "Come with me, Clotee," he said. Outside the kitchen, he whispered matter-of-factly. "The view from my room is interesting." What did he mean by that?

Tuesday, October 11, 1859

After breakfast, I slipped into Mr Harms' bedroom. Standing in the side window, I got a clear view of the woods and especially the tree where my diary and Spicy's Bible were hidden. Thanks be there were no other bedroom windows at that end of the house.

What is going on? Mr Harms knows my secret for sure. He must have seen Spicy and me at the tree when she showed me her Bible. But why didn't he tell Miz Lilly or Mas' Henley? I'm beginning to think there is more to this strange man than any of us really knows.

Later that same night

My suspicions are right. Mr Harms is not who he seems to be. When I went to move my diary from the hollow of the tree, there was a note fixed to it.

I know you can read and write.

Please be careful. I will speak to you soon.

The note was signed "H" for Harms.

I hid my diary under my dress and hurried to find Spicy. I didn't want to put her in the heat of things, but she already was. It broke my heart to tell her that Mr Harms had found her Bible. But it hurt even worser for Spicy to think I'd tattled on her. Even when I showed her how easy it was for him to see us through his window, she still didn't b'lieve me. "If that's true, then why didn't he tell Mas' Henley?"

I had no choice at that point but to 'fess everything. I took a deep breath and showed her my diary and the note Mr Harms had left. Spicy took me straight to Aunt Tee.

Daybreak Sunday, October 16, 1859

The roosters just crowed. Thank God it's Sunday and not a full workday. Aunt Tee, Spicy and me sat up all night talking. There are no secrets between us now. I'm glad in a way. In fact, I am writing in my diary right here in Aunt Tee's cabin. At first, she was 'gainst my learning – but she say now that she was just scared – didn't want me beaten or sold away. "I will not stand in the way of what might be the Lord's work being done through you, chile."

She even said for me to hide my papers in her cabin. My diary will be safe with her. I worry that I've made life unsure for Aunt Tee and Spicy. If they get caught with my papers, we could all be in sinking sand. Maybe Mr Harms will be able to help. But who is he, really? I got some ideas, but I dare not put voice to them yet.

Later

Aunt Tee and Spicy don't think I should trust Mr Harms all the way. But he hasn't done nothing to make me not trust him.

I have looked at the one-eyed man's picture over and over. He don't look at all like Mr Harms, but for after all that's been happening, I think Mr Harms might know the one-eyed man. Mr Harms isn't from the Philadelphia, the New York or the Boston. He's from Virginia. Can a southern mas'er be an abolitionist? Mr Harms said in his note that he would speak to me. Maybe I'll get answers to some of these questions then.

Monday, October 17, 1859

"Will you teach me to write my name?" Spicy asked.

I've never really thought about teaching anybody else how to write. I've always been the one learning. I used the poker to write letters in the ashes. Spicy and Aunt Tee looked on with wondering eyes. For the first time I been able to share my secret with somebody. I love seeing them smiling at the letters that makes up their names. I feel warm and good inside. What good is knowing if I cain't never use it to do some good. Spicy made an S. And Aunt Tee made a T. We've had our first lesson.

Tuesday, October 18, 1859

Mr Harms knows that I know that he knows I can read and write. But he has not said a word to me about it. Treats me the same as always. When will he speak to me?

Meanwhile, Miz Lilly aine back yet, so our housework is not as hard, but Mas' Henley's been around all week in his study. I couldn't get ink out. But Aunt Tee helped me make a mixture of charcoal ash and blackberry wine. It makes a good ink until I can do better.

Wednesday, October 19, 1859

The days are getting shorter, and it's cool in the mornings during study time. Today Mr Harms changed the study time to early afternoon when it is still hot enough to need a fanner. I would say thank you, but I dare not. He say he will speak to me, so I got to wait.

Sunday, October 23, 1859

Mas' went to fetch Miz Lilly from Richmond. We had the whole day to ourselves again. Trouble is, William wanted to come down to the Quarters to the meeting. Mr Harms thought it was a good idea. 'Course, we didn't, but what could we say?

At the meeting, Rufus talked about the three boys in the fiery furnace: Shadrach, Meshach, Abedego. Then Rufus sang a song. We all joined in. I looked over at William and Mr Harms and they were singing and clapping their hands, too.

My God's a good God. It is so.
I woke up this morning and by God's pure grace I go.
Yes, God is a great God, this I know.

We shared a table the way we always do after service. Mr Harms took William back to the house in his rolling chair. I stayed to be with Wook for a little while longer. All the smile is gone out of her eyes. I rubbed her feet, because they were so swollen. That's when she broke down and cried, saying she hated her husband, Lee. He had got a pass to visit, but came just to say he didn't love her. Lee wants to marry somebody else.

Monday, October 24, 1859

Miz Lilly is home. Lord have mercy. Mas' and Hince left the same day for races in Charleston. We all been busy washing and ironing her travel clothes – scrubbing, scrubbing. Nothing suits her. And she aine stopped going on about how filthy the house is.

Tuesday, October 25, 1859

I caught Miz Lilly in her room at a good time, and asked her if I could stay with Aunt Tee in the Quarters 'stead of in the kitchen.

I knew just how to get what I wanted out of her. I say to her, "Miz Lilly, I was thinking if you let me stay with Aunt Tee down in the Quarters, I can watch and know if somebody's talking runaway talk."

She studied on that notion. "You've never told me one thing about anybody. Why now, Clotee?"

I had to think fast and talk straight. "I figure if I help you, then you'll give me nice things like you do Missy."

That fooled her good! She let me stay in Aunt Tee's cabin, but I still got to work with Eva Mae in the kitchen and help Missy with the housework. It's a little bit like the way it used to be – Aunt Tee and Spicy and me talking all hours of the night. Now, I'll be able to write more often and not cause suspicion. It's no where near as warm or as nice as the kitchen. When I write H-O-M-E, I see here in the cabin. Home aine a place – it's a feeling of being loved and wanted. Wherever Aunt Tee and Spicy are that's home to me.

Friday, October 28, 1859

Been working all week. Today is the first time I've had a minute to write. Most nights I just fall asleep on my pallet, next to Spicy. We all too tired to talk, but it's so good being back together again under the same roof – even though it leaks.

Saturday, October 29, 1859

Aunt Tee has found a way to be useful again. She made herself a job. All the hands in the Quarters work so hard, they be too tired to cook in the evening. So, she's done started cooking for everybody. Whatever the folk can rake together, they bring it to Aunt Tee. She adds it together to make a bigger pot. They come home in the evening to a big pot. Today they had rabbit stew, wild turnips and ho'cakes fixed by the best cook in Virginia.

After last meal the same day

I picked up pieces of talk at dinner. Mr Harms was telling Miz Lilly about the Bible he'd found, but he said he found it down by the river. "Yes, Eva Mae told me you'd found a Bible and that you were trying to say it belonged to her or Clotee. Why would you think it belonged to one of the slaves and not a member of the Big House?"

"Slaves steal so badly," said Mr Harms. "When anything is missing or lost, I always begin with the house slaves. They are the ones most likely guilty."

Mr Harms was sounding like a mas'er. But when I looked closer, the Bible he showed Miz Lilly wasn't Spicy's at all. Mr Harms was helping Spicy and me, but at the same time finding favour with Miz Lilly. I felt myself smile inside.

Then Mr Harms asked if Miz Lilly knew that William has some feeling in his toes? She didn't know – she never takes time to know about such things. Mr Harms asked if he could use hot water treatments on William's legs. Say he'd learned the treatment from a doctor over in Washington.

"Only if Dr Lamb says it is all right."

Then, he asked for Missy to help him with the treatments.

"No," said Miz Lilly, "Missy is attending to me. Use Clotee."

Mr Harms knew just how to charm Miz Lilly. If he had asked for me, she never would have let me help. What is Mr Harms up to?

Monday, October 31, 1859

It's shoe-wearing time again. I hate putting on William's old hard shoes.

Eva Mae, Missy and me just about harvested everything from the house garden and preserved, pickled or dried it. The collards are ready to be picked, but Aunt Tee say wait til' the frost hits them, first. This is my favourite time of the year, when the summer heat gives way to fall coolness. I can finally get a good sleep.

Wednesday, November 2, 1859

Hince and Mas' Henley came back home winners. They also had a fine new horse, a beauty named Canterbury's Watch.

He's not as spirited as Dancer, but Hince says he's a strong runner – steady. Hince calls him "Can", because he "can run". Miz Lilly came out on the porch, took one look at the horse, stepped back inside and slammed the door.

It was good to have Hince home. Although he spends most of his time with the horses, I miss hearing him laughing and how the sound floats up to the kitchen from the stables.

I told him I was staying in Aunt Tee's cabin down in the Quarters, but I still work up in the kitchen and Big House. "I'm glad you with Aunt Tee," he said. "Somebody to see after her."

Then Hince s'prised me with a piece of red satin ribbon. It was as grand as anything Miz Lilly owned. And it was all mine. Didn't have to slip and play with it. Hince say he had bought it with money he won, betting on himself.

"I was going to wait until the Big Times to give it to you, but I couldn't wait. How do you like it?"

The word came straight from my heart and burst out of my mouth. "Beautiful!" Whenever I write B-E-A-U-T-I-F-U-L, I will see my red ribbon. It makes me feel pretty and like I want to dance and dance.

Sunday, November 6, 1859

Hince bought Spicy a measure of cloth and Aunt Tee a comb for her hair. All three of us wore our gifts to meeting. All the women in the Quarters was jealous – but Missy was so mad, she didn't stay through the whole service. Rufus talked on love.

"Love is not jealous," he said, winking at the three of us. I should have been ashamed of being so proud of my red ribbon, but I wasn't. I just held my head higher.

Monday, November 7, 1859

Missy come in the kitchen waving a white handkerchief with purple and yellow pansies on each corner. Lord, who has that girl gone and told on?

Tuesday, November 8, 1859

Missy told Miz Lilly all about the gifts Hince had bought us –
mad because he didn't bring her nothing back. Miz Lilly took
it straight to Mas' Henley.

Mas' Henley rang the plantation bell. All of us come
running to the front of the house. Mas' Henley lead us to the
stables. Oh, no. Somebody was getting ready to get a beating.

When Mas' grabbed Hince, my breath cut short.

"How'd you get money to buy gifts?" he asked Hince.

"I used the eating money you gives me to bet on myself
to win – and I winned," he say, not feeling like he'd done
no wrong.

Mas' Henley reached and got a buggy whip. "Where'd you
get the idea that you could slip behind my back and place
bets?" He told Hince to lean over and hold on to the wagon
wheel. Hince couldn't b'lieve he was getting a whupping.
Neither could I.

"But Mas', I didn't slip. I placed the bet, free and open."

Mas' Henley beat Hince. Gave him ten hard licks while
we all was made to watch. I closed my eyes and balled my
hands in a fist so tight my fingernails dug in the heel of

128

my hand. I wanted to holler out when I heard the swish of the whip hitting my brother-friend's back.

Everybody knew Hince was Mas' Henley's bread and butter – filled his pockets. If Hince got a beating, then what would ol' Mas' do if we got caught doing anything – anything. It didn't have to be wrong – just something he didn't like. Mas' Henley promised never to give Hince eating money when they was out on a trip. Say he could starve to death.

Wonder how Missy feels about herself, now? Was getting Hince a whupping worth that ugly handkerchief? We used to let Missy get away with fighting and hitting, because we thought she was pretty and all. I even wanted to be like her. But if being pretty means being that ugly inside, then Lord let me stay plain. Aunt Tee always say what go around, come around. Missy got it coming for what she did.

Wednesday, November 9, 1859

Aunt Tee took care of Hince's wounds. The buggy whip cut his skin, but not as deep as a cat-o'-nine. Hince was shamed, at first – shame of being whupped in front of everybody. Being a winning jockey didn't help him none. Mas' Henley beat him just the same.

Spicy and me tried to cheer him up by talking about Mas' Henley in the worse way. He felt some better. I could see it in his face.

One day when the abolitionists come they will stop all this beating. I wonder how far off that day is?

Friday, November 11, 1859

It rained all day — a slow rain. Turned cold afterwards. Miz Lilly called me to her room. Then we went up in the attic. There were all kinds of boxes up there — things I'd never seen before. Dresses, coats, hats. It smelled of ol' and the dust made me sneeze.

Miz Lilly opened a creaky trunk and pulled out a pair of shoes and a dress that musta b'longed to her daughter. She handed them to me. I had never had no real shoes or a pretty dress. Just the plain white pull-overs Aunt Tee stitched up for me.

"Your mama made this dress for my Clarissa when she was a girl. Now you can have it." I quick put the shoes on. They were a little big, but much softer than William's big shoes. My toes had plenty of room and the sides weren't rough and hard. I put the dress on. It felt like it had been mine all along, because Mama had made it. I buried my face in it and tried to smell Mama, but it just made me sneeze more. Miz Lilly was almost a person, but I had to keep my wits about me. She wasn't nice just to be nice. She was up to something.

When I showed Aunt Tee and Spicy what Miz Lilly had give me, they looked at me with wondering faces. "I didn't tell her nothing. Honest!" They b'lieved me, but warned me to be careful-like.

Saturday, November 12, 1859

This study season would have been over for me, because its been too cold to fan. If it hadn't been for those hot water treatments Mr Harms is giving William, my learning would have ended like before. But Mr Harms got me helping during study time. Still not a word from Mr Harms. He sees me every day, but he walks right by me. I might as well be a shadow person. Wonder will the treatments really do William any good?

Sunday, November 13, 1859

I just hurried back to Aunt Tee's cabin to write what I just seen.

I was going back to the kitchen from the Quarters a while ago, when I seen Mr Harms going into the woods. I followed him all the way down to the river, being quiet as I could. He put his hands to his mouth and made the sound of a bird. In a few minutes, I heard the same sound. Then out of the river mist stepped a ghostly-looking man. As the moon slipped from behind a cloud, I got a good look. He was the one-eyed man in the picture – the abolitionist – no ghost at all, but in the flesh.

My heart was beating in my chest so hard, I was sure they could hear it. I wanted to run out and tell the one-eyed man that he was my hero – like the long-ago Herquelez that Mr Harms had read about. I wanted to tell the one-eyed man that I was an abolitionist too, and that I wanted to get rid of slavery just like him. But I decided just to watch and listen.

I know now that Mr Harms is in with the abolitionists for sure. That means that not all abolitionists are from the Philadelphia, the New York or the Boston. They come from everywhere – even from the south – even from Virginia. If Mr Harms was an abolitionist, then what was he doing here at Belmont? Might it have something to do with slaves running away on that railroad that's underground?

Monday, November 14, 1859

Hince came to Aunt Tee's cabin after the dinner meal, none the worse for the beating he took. Licks heal fast on the outside, but they're a whole lot harder to heal inside.

We could hear Rufus singing down in the Quarters, "Coming for to carry me home."

Sunday, November 20, 1859

Today we had meeting in the Quarters same as always. I wore my new dress – Mama's dress. Everybody say how nice I looked. I tried real hard not to be puffed up, but when Missy came, I just had to strut a little. "Pride go 'fore a fall," Rufus whispered in my ear. Then he winked.

Hince came to meeting and sat 'side of Spicy. Wherever Spicy is these days, Hince aine far behind.

Rufus preached about Elijah who was taken to heaven in a fiery chariot. Home means freedom when we sing. So Rufus's story is telling us, we're going to go to freedom one day, soon. I thought about Mr Harms and the one-eyed man and the Underground Railroad. Was somebody getting ready to run?

We closed singing –

Swing low, sweet chariot.
Coming for to carry me home.
Swing low, sweet chariot.
Coming for to carry me home.
    I looked over Jordan and what did I see.
    Coming for to carry me home.
    A band of angels coming after me.
    Coming for to carry me home.
Swing low, sweet chariot.
Coming for to carry me home.
Swing low, sweet chariot.
Coming for to carry me home.

Later

Wook came to Aunt Tee's cabin late this evening to talk to us. Times had changed. We hardly knew what to say to each other any more. Wook did a good part of the talking – remembering mostly. She teased me about the time we were playing hiding, and I hid in some poison ivy. That made us all laugh. Then Wook said she had to go. "Goodbye," she say, hugging Aunt Tee and Spicy. When she hugged me, she whispered softly. "Pray for me."

I haven't said anything to anybody. But Wook is getting ready to run – and the one-eyed man and Mr Harms are probably helping her. Don't know how I know it, but I do. I do.

Monday, November 21, 1859

Things have been in an uproar all morning. Mas' Henley cain't be reasoned with. I was right! Rufus, Aggie, Wook and the baby ran away last night. They just up and flew away.

Mas' Henley made a promise. "I'll free anybody who brings me information about Rufus and who helped him. Think of it, your freedom. I swear it!"

This aine about no handkerchief. Mas' Henley is promising freedom. If I told him everything I know about Mr Harms and the one-eyed man, I could be free. Free. The idea is tempting. My God! I cain't believe I just had that thought. How could I even think of doing such a thing? I couldn't tell on Mr Harms. I know there are people here at Belmont who would turn in their dear mamas for a piece of meat, let 'lone freedom. Lord, put that ugly idea out of my mind forever and ever. Amen.

Tuesday, November 22, 1859

Mas' Henley and a group of men went out looking for Rufus and his family. Rufus was the only person who has ever dared to run away from Belmont and we wanted him to make it, even though we couldn't say it – not even to each other. There was lots of singing about heaven – but we all know heaven is freedom.

Our hopes were crushed like fall leaves 'neath our feet when Mas' Henley got back this evening. Mas' Henley called all of us to him. He threw bloody pants and a shirt on the ground before us. "They're dead." He spat out the words like bad fruit. "All 'em. We had to shoot Rufus. The others drowned in the river, when the boat they was in turned over. Current took them under."

Rufus? Aggie? Wook? Baby Noah – all dead! What happened to the railroad that takes slaves to freedom? Didn't the one-eyed man help Rufus and his family?

From this day forward Mas' Henley say we aine 'llowing no more Sunday meetings, and we cain't speak of Rufus or any members of his family. Mas' might be able to tell us what we can do with our bodies, but he cain't tell me what to feel, what to think. I will remember Rufus and his family as long as I live – and he cain't stop me!

Later that same night

Even though Mas' Henley has forbidden us to gather, we mourned the loss of our friends in our own way. We raised our voices in song from our cabins in the Quarters, from the orchards and kitchen, wherever we were. We didn't need to be together to share our grief. We sang our hurt. We clapped our sorrow. We never spoke their names, but we all knew we were mourning our own, Rufus and Aggie, Wook and little Noah. They were free at last. . .

> *I got a robe, you got a robe,*
> *All of God's chullun got a robe.*
> *When I get to hea'vn, gon' to put on my robe*
> *And shout all over God's hea'vn.*
> *Hea'vn. Hea'vn. Everybody's talkin' 'bout hea'vn*
> *Aine goin' there.*
> *Hea'vn. I'm going to shout all over God's hea'vn.*

Wednesday, November 23, 1859

We woke this morning and the world looked like it's done been covered in a thin white veil. The first hard frost. Slaughtering time.

Saturday, November 26, 1859

The men slaughtered hogs for days. The smell of fresh animal blood turns my stomeck, so I stayed clear of the slaughtering yard and stayed close to the kitchen where pots and pans clanked and banged. The noise helped drown out the sound of dying.

As I write, the smokehouse is filled to overflowing with hams and sausage, bacon and ribs – all slow-curing in smoke from smouldering wood chips.

Later

Aunt Tee say just when you think you know the devil, he changes his face. Now I know what she means. I've always thought Mas' Henley was the worse man in the world. But then come Briley Waith. Rufus was always in charge of slaughtering, but Mas' Henley hired Briley Waith to take charge this year. He's common as dirt, tall and lean with sun-red skin. Keeps a tangle of white hair hid under a beat-up hat. The cat-o'-nine that hangs to Mr Waith's side tells me he's a man who keeps it close, because he plans to use it.

Watching Waith makes me feel sick in my heart. There is something 'bout him that frightens me way down deep inside. We made soap today under his watchful eyes. He sees everything. To me he's a dangerment – like a snake, sly.

Sunday, November 27, 1859

Thank goodness for good days – they take the sting out of the bad ones. Aunt Tee sent me down to the stables to get Hince. When we walked into the cabin it was filled with the smell of cinnamon and apples. For days, I've been slipping sugar, butter, flour, lard – careful not to get caught. Today I got the cinnamon stick – enough to make a small apple pie.

It's first frost – Hince's birthtime. "Just for you," I say, giving him a shiny black button I had found and polished. He promised to keep it always and I knew he would.

"I don't have nothing to give," say Spicy. She stood toe to toe, eye to eye with him. Then she gave him a kiss, right on the mouth. "I'm glad you was born."

He let out a whoop that could be heard clear down to the

river. We all had to laugh.

At times like these we missed Uncle Heb. But while Spicy and I worked on the quilt, we told stories about him, and about Rufus and Aggie and Wook. That made us more thankful that we were together. Apple pie has never tasted so good.

Monday, November 28, 1859

Just as we feared, Mas' Henley liked Waith enough to keep him on. Pulled several men 'way from the tobacco drying sheds and put them on the job of building Mr Waith's overseer's cabin. Mas' Henley chose a spot that gave him clear view of the whole plantation. He can see the Quarters out his back door and the back of the Big House from his front door. From the left side window Waith can see the kitchen and the fields behind, and from his right side window Waith can see the orchards and woods. Clear to me, Mas' Henley has brought Waith here to be his eyes.

Tuesday, November 29, 1859

Miz Lilly sent for me today. She was lying in bed – say she had a fever.

"So you like your shoes?" she say, groaning softly. I offered to get her some water. She called to me to stand closer. Then she grabbed my hand.

"You like nice things, don't you?" I say yes, then she come back with, "You can have lots of things, but you've got to tell me what I want." She asked me question after question about Mr Harms – so many my head went to swimming. But I was real careful not to let on to nothing. Wonder what's got her sniffing around Mr Harms like a ol' hound dog. Missy must have brought her a bone. Now she wants me to bring her another one. I say, "If I hear or see something, Miz Lilly, I'll come to you right now." All the time I'm thinking, "I'd never tell you a thing – 'specially not on a abolitionist."

Wednesday, November 30, 1859

All this time has passed and Mr Harms still aine talked to me. But things have changed so much, I need to tell him Miz Lilly is trying to find something on him. But it's like I aine even in the room. During lesson time, I rub William's legs after they been soaked in hot, hot water. I'm still listening and learning all I can, but I wish Mr Harms would talk to me.

Thursday, December 1, 1859

While serving the noon meal, I heard Miz Lilly tell Mas' Henley that she had written to a friend of hers in Washington. The friend had wrote back saying, "Mr Harms's father and mother are well-bred southerners, but his uncles Josiah and Joshua Harms are hell-bent abolitionists." She sucked in as though she had spoken a word purely evil. "Who is this Mr Harms?" she say.

This I know, Mas' and Miz Henley fights on just about

everything in the world, 'cept'n slavery. On that notion they are together. They plenty mad about losing Rufus and his family. Mas' Henley say he would speak to Mr Harms 'bout his family.

I know Mr Harms said he would speak to me, but that was weeks ago. He never has. I got to warn him, so I'm just gon' have to speak to him first.

Friday, December 2, 1859

I took a big, big chance today. I waited outside William's room before class. When Mr Harms came down the hall, I whispered. "Be careful. They know 'bout your uncles being abolitionists. They think you might be one, too." Mr Harms never said a word to me – never even looked my way. I wonder did he hear me?

Later

Mr Harms heard me all right. After supper, he told Mas'
Henley about his uncles being abolitionists. It was smart for
him to bring it up, before he got asked about it. I was serving
them coffee in the large parlour when I heard Mr Harms say
he was sick 'shamed of his relations and wanted to forget
they was ever kin. That seemed to set well with Mas' Henley.
I found every reason to stay in that parlour listening. I poked
up the fire as Mas' Henley was saying, "I'm trusting you to be
an honourable man while you're an employee in my home."
Coming from Mas' Henley it sounded like a warning. I never
took my eyes off Miz Lilly. She didn't say much. But the
compression on her face told the whole story. She didn't trust
Mr Harms not a stitch. He's got an enemy in Miz Lilly – and
I think he knows it.

Saturday, December 3, 1859

They finished Mr Waith's house today. Hince say he's so glad Waith is not staying in the stables with him any more, because he snored so bad.

Waith's got a two room log cabin – one room and a sleeping loft – complete with a front and back door and four windows. Nothing special, but the way he's carrying on, you'd think it was a Big House. Miz Lilly helped furnish his place with leftovers from the attic. Mas' Henley gave him the key to the storehouse and made him welcome.

Aunt Tee say Waith is po' white trash that aine never had it so good. That means he's gon' want to make sure he pleases Mas' and Miz Henley, to keep what he's got. I plan to stay clear of the man – he scares me.

Before going to bed, I looked out the window and saw smoke coming from Waith's chimney. The overseer has settled in for a long winter's stay at Belmont. A cold chill went up my back.

Sunday, December 4, 1859

The wind woke me up, whistling through the cracks in the cabin wall. Sounds like whisperings from the strange dream I was having. Trying, now, to write it down while I remember it. Even so it is hard to put the pieces together. I am running, running fast, but I don't know where I'm going. I see Hince being taken away in chains – Aunt Tee is begging Mr Harms to help him, but he won't talk to her. He won't talk to me. I see a sign that says the Philadelphia, and another that says the New York, and another that says the Boston. People with no faces are holding up signs that say "We are abolitionists." I'm running to them, but I never get closer.

Sitting here in the cold darkness, I've made up my mind that I'm going to speak to Mr Harms. I've just got to figure out how and where I can do it.

Monday, December 5, 1859

Mr Harms and I see each other during lessons every day, but we never have time alone.

I have to say this for William, he's trying really, really hard with his lessons. No whining when I rub his legs either. I know the water is hot, and the exercises are hard for him, but he never fails to try. And today for all of his hard work, William wiggled his big toe. It was a small thing, but it made me feel big inside – good – like I'd had a part in making it happen by rubbing his legs and feet every day. It was like doctoring. I know how Aunt Tee and Spicy must feel when they help bring a new life into the world.

Tuesday, December 6, 1859

Samella, a barn cat, had a litter of three kittens under the kitchen porch. Two died. I captured the last one, a jet black one, and took it to William. I'd never heard William say thank you for anything in his life, but he thanked me for the kitten. He named it Shadow.

Later

"That was a kind thing you did for William," said Mr Harms. He was standing in the doorway to the study. "Keep dusting."

At last, we were having that talk. My head was spinning with thoughts. What to ask? What to say? "I've been waiting and waiting for this time."

Our talk went like this:

"I had to make sure you could be trusted – and that you could trust me."

"Are you a abolitionist?" I wanted to know that in the worst way.

He smiled, but his eyes were serious. "Yes, I am. Who else knows about me?"

"Aunt Tee, Spicy and me. But Miz Lilly's looking at you real careful-like."

"Thanks for the warning. She could be a problem."

"Are you and the one-eyed man the Underground Railroad?"

"No. Not by ourselves," he whispered. "We are conductors."

He told me it was neither underground nor a railroad. It's a group of people who work together to help slaves get to freedom.

"You can read and write. I figured you learned by listening during lessons. Remarkable."

"I done learned a lot from you." Then I say, "You a southerner. Why you want to end slavery?"

He wasn't able to answer, because somebody was coming. I had more questions to ask. Later. Now it's time to take Miz Lilly her warm milk before bedtime. I got to be sure that I don't give away nothing in my face.

Wednesday, December 7, 1859

Today, Dr Lamb came to see William – said he was improving. That still gave Mr Harms and me a moment to talk. He told me Belmont was the first station on the Underground Railroad in this area. It was a low point in the river, where it narrows and the current is less swift. Runaways meet their first conductor here in the Belmont woods and are taken to the next point.

Why couldn't poor Rufus and his family make it?

Thursday, December 8, 1859

The days are short and cold. The fields have been laid by. Tobacco is yellowing over slow coals. Waith's put everybody to work fixing up the place for Christmas – the Big Times. Another holiday. Endless chores.

Eva Mae is making fruit cakes today. I chopped nuts and berries 'til my fingers have got no feeling. Missy got on one of Clarissa's old dresses – Miz Lilly probably promised her a hat, too, if she tells on me. Missy and me hardly talk any more except when we serving the food. She hangs under Miz Lilly like Shadow does William.

Friday, December 9, 1859

We spent the day in the barn, re-stuffing Miz Lilly's mattress with fresh down we've been saving all year.

Hince has been coming to Aunt Tee's cabin every night to sit with Spicy, so I can't write until he leaves.

Since our talk in the study, Mr Harms has been slipping me things to read. I hide them under my dress until I get here. I read the papers to Aunt Tee and Spicy. A lot of it we don't understand, but a lot of my questions have answers now.

Abolitionists live everywhere, just like I thought. But, what makes me happyest is that some abolitionists are women and some are even people who done been slaves, just like me. Mr Harms say that a used-to-be-slave named Frederick Douglass teached himself to read and write just like me. Now he's a abolitionist and writes his own newspaper up in the New York called The North Star. I want to read that paper some day. Maybe I will. I know I will.

Saturday, December 10, 1859

Aunt Tee sent Spicy and me to pick the last of the beets from the house garden. They're tender and sweet after the frost hits the ground. On the way back from the garden Waith jumped out and grabbed Spicy's arm. "You're right pretty for a black gal," he say, spitting tobacco juice.

He hissed at me to git, but I wouldn't go – not without Spicy. I held on to her hand. He snapped his whip in my direction. "Git like I tol' you, or I'll give you a whupping gal!"

"Mr Harms wouldn't like you bothering Spicy. He done picked her for hisself." I surprised myself at how fast I could speak a lie. It was a good lie, because it was helping Spicy. She was frozen in fear, because she knew Waith didn't have nothing good in mind. Waith b'lieved me. He let Spicy go, and we ran as fast as we could to Aunt Tee.

I'll tell Mr Harms what I said, and maybe he can protect Spicy until . . . until what? Dare I write it? Until we run away!

Sunday, December 11, 1859

I miss the good Sundays we had when Rufus was here. But Mr Harms gave Spicy's Bible back. He had been keeping it in his room where it would be safe. The one he showed Miz Lilly was one of his. Spicy was thankful to get it back – it being her mama's and all. Now I read to Spicy and Aunt Tee when we get a chance.

Later

There was a big celebration at Belmont tonight. Had to work in the kitchen. Mr Cleophus Tucker and the other men Mas' Henley supported won. The house looked beautiful, everything shining and sparkling. We'd worked hard enough to make it look that way. The guests went on and on about how they hate abolitionists and northern meddlers. Made me smile inside, seeing Mr Harms right in the middle of them – and they don't even know he was a fox in the henhouse.

Mas' Edmund Ruffin was part of the group tonight. He was the one who talked the longest and the loudest about the rights of slaveholders. He was always talking 'bout his freedom. "We are a free nation. We fought England for our freedom. We will fight again for our freedom if we must!"

Mas'ers talk a powerful lot when it comes to their freedom. But when it comes to freeing the slaves – they gets struck deaf and dumb.

Monday, December 12, 1859

It's night. It was cold all morning, warmed up by late afternoon, and now it is cold again – a winter cold. Long hard day over. Miz Lilly fussed around in the kitchen most of the morning – setting up for the big Christmas dinner. She ended up slapping Eva Mae twice 'fore it was over.

Later, Miz Lilly gave every one in the Quarters a measure of cloth to make something for the coming Big Times. I gave my piece to Aunt Tee, because I got Mama's dress to wear. Aunt Tee is stitching up something real special while Spicy and me work on our quilt. We almost got it finished.

The cabin floor is cold, so we keep our feet wrapped in rags. We sit by the fire, so our fronts are warm, but our backs are cold. There are so many cracks in the walls, the wind whistles. And it's also getting harder and harder for Aunt Tee to piece a meal together, even though I'm slipping as much as I can out of the kitchen. Winter hard times is upon us. What keeps us going is waiting on the Big Times – our Week of Sundays. Uncle Heb always used to say, if we can last through February we can March on through.

Tuesday, December 13, 1859

Riders woke us at daybreak. Dogs barking. Torches glowing in the darkness. Aunt Tee, Spicy and I went to the door to see who it was. Late-night riders always mean one thing – trouble.

The lead rider, Wilson, spoke first. He was quick to the point. "Two of my nigras have run away – a buck named Raf and a mulatto gal named Cora Belle. We beat it out of the gal's mama that the two was helped by a white man, what's missing an eye. If we catch him, he's gon' lose more'n a eye." The men reined their horses. "We aim to hang him."

"The dogs traced them here to your orchards. We'd like to go in, with your permission," said Higgins.

Mas' Henley raised a fist. "You have my permission. And if you'll let me dress, I'll go with you."

"Me, too," said Mr Waith, bursting out of his cabin. "Chasing and catching runaways is what I been doing for the last three years."

I knew he was something like that – a low-lifed slave-chaser.

Wednesday, December 14, 1859

Mas' Henley come back from the hunt, telling us how they found the runaways. "We hung 'em," he hissed angrily. "My offer still stands," he said. "Freedom to the one who gives me any information about this one-eyed white man. Think about it – freedom." So they hadn't caught the one-eyed man.

I just scratched F-R-E-E-D-O-M in the ashes. I still don't get no picture. Freedom is a hard word to understand.

Thursday, December 15, 1859

Waith been pushing everybody to get Belmont cleaned up for the Big Times. After what happened with the runaways we been moving real slow-like – got no joy in our souls.

Women from the Quarters been up in the kitchen to help Eva Mae with the early cooking and cleaning. I helped put the big rug out of the large parlour and beat all the dust out of it. I got to coughing and couldn't stop. Aunt Tee made me some syrup out of honey and herbs and I finally stopped.

Later

When I went to the stables to take Hince a plate of food, Mr Harms pulled me aside. I almost screamed, thinking it was that nasty Waith.

"Got news," he say. "Those runaways aren't dead. They just tell you runaways are dead, so you'll be afraid to run."

"Does that mean Rufus and Aggie?" I was so hoping. But Mr Harms say, no they didn't make it. Rufus wasn't willing to trust the Underground Railroad plan. "He never quite b'lieved that a southern man could be as against slavery as I am. But there are plenty of us." Rufus had tried to make it on his own.

"Some runaways make it alone," Mr Harms s'plained. "They need help most times. Lots of help. I tried to help Rufus – talked to him several times when I heard he was planning a run. Rufus never really trusted me."

What happened to Rufus and his family should never happen to another family. One of them might have made it if they could swim. Mas' Henley won't let us learn how to swim, because he knows, if we stay stupid he can keep us. Come spring, I'm learning how to swim – just in case I ever need to know how.

I forgot to tell Mr Harms about the lie I told Waith to save Spicy. I've got to remember.

Friday, December 16, 1859

Rained all day – a slow cold rain. Miserable. I sat with William in his room for a while. We played with Shadow. I pumped his legs, up and down, up and down, keeping them moving. Sadly, the hot water treatments aine helped more than to get a few toes a-going. The rest of him is still the same – nothing near walking. He's in mighty good spirits though – giggling all the time. Maybe it's the Big Times that's making him so happy. Dr Lamb visited yesterday. Stayed for dinner. Company – even company as nice as Dr Lamb, always means more work for us in the kitchen.

Saturday, December 17, 1859

Mr Harms still treats me like I'm not there when others be around us.

He left me a copy of The Liberator, put out by a abolitionist named William Lloyd Garrison from the Boston. I read the pages to Aunt Tee and Spicy. They listened to every word – stories about black abolitionists.

I read about a woman named Sojourner Truth, who speaks out against slavery everywhere she goes. Even when the mas'ers say they gon' stone her to death, she keeps a-talking. Aine scared of nothing, because she's telling the truth. "Slavery must be destroyed – root and branch!"

I am so glad to know about Miz Sojourner. I mean to be like her one day. Maybe even meet her when I get to freedom. Maybe we could be abolitionists together. Demagine that. But will I be brave like the shepherd boy, David? If I was with Miz Sojourner, she'd help me be strong – and we can end slavery, too.

Sunday, December 18, 1859

Waith works the people in the Quarters like dogs, won't let
up on them a minute – push, work, driving night and day –
painting, chopping winter wood, feeding the livestock, on
and on. He's constantly yelling and screaming and lashing
that whip. I'd like to wrap it around his neck and give it a
good yank! The more he yells the more Mas' Henley and the
Missus feel they're getting their money's worth.

Monday, December 19, 1859

It snowed today, not enough to cover the ground. William
sat by the window and longed to play once more in the snow.

"You're different, Clotee," William say matter-of-fact-like.
Lord, now William is noticing me. Who next?

I made on like I didn't know what he was talking about.
He say, "You don't sound like the other slaves. You say talking,
instead of talkin'. You say, I am instead of I is. You say, they

161

were instead of they was – and things like that. You talk almost as good as a white person. Why is that?"

I shrugged my shoulders and got out of there as quick as I could. Missy was always teasing me about talking proper. Miz Lilly had spoke about it, too, and now William. Was my learning to be my undoing? I must be particular to write but not talk too proper. I could get myself into trouble.

Tuesday, December 20, 1859

Five days to the Big Times.

Two men by the name of Campbelle came to Belmont today. They stayed for supper. The older Campbelle is gray-haired with a matching moustache, stocky, but well-dressed. The son is taller, thinner. The Campbelles are horsemen from Tennessee, same as Mas' Henley.

While serving biscuits and coffee, I turned to listening. I'm piecing it all together so I can write it down.

"We've been watching you for some time," said Silas Campbelle, the older man. "We like the way your boy rides."

"I got the best jockey in Virginia right here at Belmont," Mas' Henley bragged.

"He'd be great if he had a fair mount," said Amos Campbelle, the son. "We've got the right horse. We need your jockey."

"What's your offer?"

"We'd like to buy Hince."

My heart sank! I almost dropped the plate of dessert tea cakes, but I caught them before they all slide off the tray and on the floor. The men were too fixed on what they were saying to pay attention to me.

"No deal," Mas' Henley answered. "But, I'll make this bet. My jockey against your horse. I lose, you take Hince. I win, I take your horse."

"Set the date?"

"New Year's Day."

Later

Hince was shocked when I told him what I'd overheard.

"So Mas' Henley done bet on me 'gainst the Campbelles' horse?" He shrugged and went back to rubbing Can. Is that all Mas' Henley thought of Hince – to bet him against a horse?

"S'pose you lose?" I asked.

Hince talked brave. "I won't lose. Big Can is a good horse,

nobody really knows how good. Mas' Henley musta planned this all along. That's why he been having me hold back a little, winning without ever letting Can stretch out. That's gon' be our edge on the Campbelles."

Once he put voice to those words Hince didn't seem worried. All I pray for is for him to be right. So does Aunt Tee and most especially Spicy. Hince can't lose.

Thursday, December 22, 1859

We all gathered on the porch to see the Christmas tree lights. The tree didn't look as pretty to me as it used to. Maybe Waith being here has spoiled the Big Times for us all.

As hard as everybody done worked to get the place ready for the holidays, Briley Waith went to Mas' Henley and tried to get our off-days cut short. I heard him say with all the runaways happening, he thinks we should be kept bent over working so we can't take time to study up on freedom.

Thank goodness, Mas' Henley had sense enough to realize that he'd have a r'bellion on his hands if he didn't give us the days off between Christmas and New Year's.

"Tell you what, though," he told Waith. "I won't give out any travel passes this year. That ought to cut back on any runaway attempts. Thank you for thinking ahead, Waith. You're a good man."

I just wrote M-E-A-N in the ashes. Mean. The picture of Waith is clear in my head. This is going to be a sad, sad Christmas for folks who were hoping for passes to visit their loved ones on nearby plantations.

Saturday, December 24, 1859 – Christmas Eve

Been so busy, I aine had a chance to write in a few days. Everything is ready for the Big Times – in the Big House and down here in the Quarters. Even the weather is on our side. If it stays warm like it is today, we'll get to eat our dinner outside.

Everybody is home for the holidays. Mr Harms stayed here, rather than go to his home. Clarissa and her husband are here from Richmond. The tree is up, the stockings are hung, and we've got the cream ready for Mas' Henley's famous eggnog.

The Missus led the family in singing carols. As soon as I could slip away, I joined Aunt Tee and Spicy in the stables. That's where the folks from the Quarters were having their

Christmas Eve dance. All under the watchful eyes of Waith, the overseer.

Aunt Tee served him a glass of danderlion wine. Waith drank it and ate a big plate of pickled pig feet, a roasted sweet potato and ashcake. Aunt Tee winked at Spicy and me, because she had put a potion in his drink.

'Fore long, we looked for Waith. He was curled up like a fat snake, sound asleep. Slept through the whole party. He never guessed what had made him so sleepy. Thank goodness for Aunt Tee's potions – and the Afric woman that gave her the recipe.

Sunday, December 25, 1859 – Christmas Day

It is Christmas – all day. "Christmas gif'," we all shouted outside Mas' Henley's window first thing this morning. After the families from the Quarters came to the Big House to greet the family and get their gifts, they hurried back to the Quarters to begin their Week of Sundays. Us who work in the kitchen had to work all day – fetching and toting, wiping and cleaning.

Missy saw another side of Miz Lilly today. Missy was

moving slow-like and whining about having to work on Christmas. All at once Miz Lilly popped Missy right upside the head. It hurt Missy's heart that I saw her get slapped.

I had Aunt Tee and Spicy bent over laughing, when I told her how Missy looked – eyes all bucked, mouth poked out – what a sight. She had it coming after what she did to Hince.

Later

Everybody in the Big House is happy because William stood up on his own today. I felt good seeing him standing up all by hisself, too. So that's why he's been all happy. He knew about this. Mr Harms got lots of praise. Even Miz Lilly had to 'fess that Mr Harms had helped her son stand. He'll be taking a few steps any day now.

I feel happy for William. I'd helped William come this far, too. I'd rubbed his legs and toes and sat with him when he was lonely. Nobody knew what I'd done – but I knew and that made me feel well within myself.

Monday, December 26, 1859

Today begins the first day of the Big Times. No work for the field hands. For us in the kitchen double work – more toting, fetching. Yesterday after we had served the big meal for the Henleys and cleaned up, we went down to the barn where there was a gathering going on.

Aunt Tee had made a cake from stuff I'd been sneaking out of the kitchen for weeks. All the elder folk stood to one side as judges. Somebody started patting the juba, clapping the tune. Then came the couples, strutting the cakewalk. Hince and Spicy come out first – high-stepping and kicking their heels. They were wearing matching shirts that Aunt Tee had made from the cloth Miz Lilly handed out. Everybody had to say they were a fine-looking couple. But they could also dance.

I had on my dress that Mama had made and the ribbon that Hince had brought me. Missy had on one of Clarissa's dresses, too. But mine was better – because Mama had made mine.

Aunt Tee 'llowed that I could dance the cakewalk this year with a boy other than Hince. Me and Buddy Barnes, Miz Clarissa's carriage driver, stepped together. He swung me up and swung me down – from side to side and up the middle.

"You look mighty nice, Clotee," Buddy Barnes said. My face turned hot and my head topped light – as light as my feet felt dancing with Buddy Barnes. As long as I live I will never, ever forget dancing with Buddy Barnes – even though Spicy and Hince were the cakewalk winners. They each took a slice of the cake for themselves, then they let everybody else have a bite.

Of course Missy was a sore loser – but she only makes herself look bad – keep pushing, pushing. Everybody knows how Spicy and Hince feel about each other. Missy should just give up.

Friday, December 30, 1859

The Week of Sundays has gone so fast. Like most holidays it's been filled with work – up the stairs, down the stairs. Bring me this, Clotee. Take that there, Clotee. Clotee. Clotee. I wish I could change my name. It is always late when we finish. Eva Mae was so tired this evening, she just fell fast asleep up in the attic. I eased out of the kitchen without waking her.

Saturday, December 31, 1859 – New Year's Eve

In the Big House all the talk is about the race tomorrow. The Campbelles are here with their horse and rider. Their horse looks like a real champion – named Betty's Son. The rider is the size of a boy, but he has a lot of years in his face. I heard one of the Campbelles call him Josh.

Later

The Campbelles brought along three of their slaves who stayed in the stables with Hince. They also made good dance partners for us. Missy took one look at the young man named Booker and claimed him for the rest of the evening. Aunt Tee called her a shameless hussy. I danced with the one named Obie. He was fun and had a happy laugh, but he wasn't near as good a dancer as Buddy Barnes. The one named Shad seemed shy – didn't dance, didn't talk. He left before the party ended.

After one of the dances the straw in the barn started me to sneeze. It always makes me sneeze and cough. Aunt Tee took me outside to get some fresh air – and sent me to the cabin to get some cough syrup. When I passed the stables, I saw Shad standing at Big Can's stall.

Sunday, January 1, 1860 – New Year's Day

My God. Hince lost the race!

As best I can tell, this is what happened.

This morning it was bright and sunny, but cold – not a cloud in the sky. The course was from Belmont's front steps down to the road and back, past the Big House, down to the river and back again – about a half mile.

Carriages full of people began gathering on the grounds all morning. Hundreds were here by mid-morning. A few minutes before noon, Hince walked Can up from the stables. I could tell something was wrong with the horse. Can looked spooked, jumpy, hard to handle. I caught a look of worry in Hince's face. That spooked me.

At exactly noon, the gun fired and Can reared up, losing time that he was never able to catch up. The other horse won!

We all were too shocked to believe what our eyes had seen. Hince wasn't supposed to lose.

Right away, Hince commenced to hollering that Can had been drugged. He was right. And I knew who had done it. Shad! "I seen him at Big Can's stall last night." I went running to Mas' Henley, all the time pointing a finger at Shad. He glared at me. "Please save Hince," I begged. "Shad did something to Can, I know he did. I seen him, honest!"

"I seen him, too," said Aunt Tee. "Left the dance early last night." Shad didn't say anything. The Campbelles stayed calm.

Everybody started talking to one another, whispering about what had happened during the race. The Campbelles called for several men – all good horsemen to check out Big Can. Rouse Mosby and Len Beans checked out Can. They said there were no signs of the horse being drugged. "Were they blind?" Can wasn't acting hisself. Anybody could see that – who wanted to see it.

The next few seconds were like hours. The Campbelles claimed that the race was fair and they had won the bet. The crowd agreed and sent up a cheer.

"You've cheated me, Amos Campbelle – you have, but I can't prove it," Mas' Henley said real angry-like. Then he ordered them off his property.

The Campbelles tipped their hats and said they had other business in the area before going home. Say they'll be coming in several weeks to pick up Hince.

"Please do something, Miz Lilly," I begged her. "I saw Shad in the barn doing something to Can. He did. Please help Hince. Please don't let them take him away. Please."

Miz Lilly snatched me by the arm and pushed me toward the house. "Hush all that crying, before I give you something to cry for. You'll say anything to save Hince." Through my tears I could see her mean eyes, and I knew she wasn't about to help Hince. She was happy to be rid of him. It's hard trying not to hate Miz Lilly – but I do hate the cruelness that lives inside her.

Later

Hince been like a wild man – walking, walking, never stopping. Say he aine going with the Campbelles. Spicy been crying all day, limp with crying. "I hope Hince don't try nothing foolish like running away," say Aunt Tee. I hope not either. I got to do something, but what? What good is know-how if you can't use it when you need it. I got reading and writing, but it can't help Hince. I feel like my head is in the big mouth of the lion, but I've got to be like Daniel. Be not afraid.

Thursday, January 5, 1860

It finally happened! Mr Harms done been found out. Hince tattled. How did he know?

Later

We're all here at Aunt Tee's cabin. I'm trying to write down all that's been going on, so we'll never disremember.

Spicy told Hince about me, Mr Harms, the one-eyed man, the abolitionists – everything. She asked me to forgive her. "I trusted Hince. I didn't know he was gon' tell on po' Mr Harms."

I wouldn't a-counted Hince 'mongst the tattlers either. It breaks my heart that he has.

Would he tell on me if he got scared enough?

Still later

Hince came to Aunt Tee's cabin after the last meal, when he knew all of us would be here. "I aine going to the Deep South with the Campbelles. Why should I care about a white man? It's his life or mine." Them words didn't sound like Hince. He must be plenty scared. I would be – having to go to the Deep South.

Aunt Tee never stopped stirring the pot. She spoke. "Going to freedom this way would be a bitter road. Mr Harms may be white but he come here to help the likes of us. Wrong for one of us to be the cause of his undoing."

"What am I s'posed to do?"

"You've got to make this thing right, somehow." Then with pleading in her voice, Aunt Tee went on saying, "Oh, son, if you gets to freedom, don't let it be on a river of innocent blood – or you'll sour yo' heart and soul."

Hince dropped his head. "I aine going to the Deep South and that's all there is to it. I'm purely sorry 'bout Mr Harms, but it's him or me, and right now, I got to look out after me." He looked at Spicy. She didn't say nothing.

I stood with Aunt Tee. "Mr Harms could have turned me

in to win favour with Miz Lilly and Mas' Henley. He never did. I owe him something. I'm gon' try to help."

Now that I've studied on it a spell, I can't shake a stick at Hince without it pointing back at me. I told on Shad when I thought it would save Hince. And I didn't care. Now Hince done used what he knew to bargain with Mas' Henley for his freedom. He aine about to go to the Deep South. I understand wanting to be free, but telling on Mr Harms aine the way to do it – it just aine right.

Right now I feel like we're the Israelites standing at the Red Sea. Pharaoh's army is coming in chariots. Our backs are to the water. Mr Harms is tied up in the study waiting for the sheriff to come. What we need is for God to push back the waters so we can cross over on dry land. We need a plan.

Friday, January 6, 1860

We've got a plan that might save Mr Harms. It may or may not work, but we've got to try to save him. We can't just let him die. God, please help us like you did the three boys in the fiery furnace.

Saturday, January 7, 1860

I'm still shaking from the cold and fear. It snowed all night, so the sheriff didn't get here until this afternoon. This is what happened.

The sheriff and Waith came to the Big House. Spicy and me slipped in the side door and hid in the pantry where we could see and hear everything that was going on in the large parlour of the Big House. If Mr Harms was afraid, he didn't show it. He looked as strange and out of order as he did the first day I laid eyes on him – not at all like the picture of a brave and daring abolitionist.

Just like we'd planned it back at the cabin – Hince said that he had seen Mr Harms talking to the one-eyed man down by the river. "The same one-eyed man who's been helping slaves get away." Hince did a fine job.

Mr Harms said none of it was true. "I don't know a one-eyed man." That was good. We 'spected he'd say that.

Then it was time for Spicy to come in. She was so nervous, I had to push her two times. But she burst into the room, screaming, "Oh, please, Mas' Henley, don't hurt Mr Harms. He aine done nothing wrong. Hince be just lying 'cause he's jealous – jealous of me . . . and Mr Harms. Tell 'em, Hince. Tell 'em." Spicy was even better than when we practiced it in the cabin. I prayed Mr Harms would catch on to what we were doing. I had never gotten around to telling him what I'd told Waith about him and Spicy.

"No, I'm the one telling the truth," Hince say, right on time.

The room fell quiet. Mas' Henley's mouth fell open. You could have pushed Miz Lilly over with a broom straw.

"Here at Belmont? I'm so ashamed," she say, heaving a big sigh. Mr Harms stood still and quiet.

The sheriff shifted around from foot to foot. "We got two nigras with two different stories. How do we get at the truth. Have you and this gal been together?"

Mr Harms wouldn't answer. Waith leaned over to Mas' Henley. "Well, I heard that Harms had picked that one out for hisself." This part was going just as we had hoped. What happened next took me by surprise.

"Spicy is telling the truth," William shouted from the doorway. "I've seen her go into Mr Harms's room many times. I also heard Spicy and Hince having a fight in the stables. Maybe Hince is jealous and isn't telling the truth."

That was all we needed – two white men's word – no matter if one was a boy. The sheriff untied Mr Harms, saying he would not take Mr Harms – not enough evidence.

Now it was my time to heave a sigh. We'd done it! We'd saved Mr Harms. I felt just like we'd killed Goliath.

Later

When the sheriff was gone, Mas' Henley slapped Spicy so hard she fell and slid across the room, bumping her head 'gainst the wall. I think Spicy is the bravest person in the whole wide world for doing what she did. She's braver than Sojourner Truth and all the abolitionists rolled together. Spicy knew she was probably going to get punished in a bad way, but she was willing to go under the lash to save Mr Harms's life. I saw Hince close his eyes and clench his fists. He was at that jumping over spot. I was praying that he wouldn't jump over.

See, I remember when Mr Barclay's Kip crossed over. He went wild on his mas'er, took the whip away and beat his own mas'er with it. They hung Kip, but he died smiling. Sometimes, I guess people get tired of being hit on, beat on, mistreated. I reckon people get tired of seeing they loved ones smacked in the face – half fed – worked near 'bout to death. I saw Hince come mighty close to that jumping over spot, when Mas' Henley hit Spicy that hard. But he held hisself, because the plan was working.

Mr Harms didn't make a move. He hardly looked like he was breathing. I don't think I was breathing, either.

"What kind of southern-born man are you?" Mas' Henley asked, spitting out the angry words. "You come in my house and use one of my girls, and then turn around and rob me of my property? Steal my property away on some blasted Underground Railroad?"

"I am a tutor, sir—"

"No. No," Mas' say, cutting in. "I believe Hince told me the truth."

That's what I was waiting to hear. Now I could breathe.

"You know how I know? Hince doesn't want to leave Belmont – his only home. You abolitionists don't understand and you never will. Our slaves love us. They run away when you people come down here exciting them about freedom – freedom to do what? They are like children – unable to do for themselves."

Hince and Mr Harms wisely said nothing. They let Mas' Henley rattle on, fooling himself into b'lieving we slaves was happy to be slaves.

Then Miz Lilly stood up. "You helped my son. That's why I stopped my husband from killing you. So, the best thing for you to do, sir, is get off Belmont and before I reconsider." Then Miz Lilly swished away.

So far our plan had worked – all of it.

Late Saturday night

William and I were the only ones standing on the porch – cold, but huddled together, watching Mr Harms load his buggy. All three of us knew that William had lied to save Mr Harms. He had not seen Spicy, because she had never been to Mr Harms's room. He had not seen Hince and Spicy fussing because they had never had a fuss. William knows that I know he lied – but we will never speak of it, I'm sure.

It's natural-like for William to be sad. Mr Harms was above all else a very good teacher. Waith stood by a pile of books in the drive. He pointed the shotgun at Mr Harms's head while the teacher climbed into the buggy. "Please, may I have my books. Why burn them?"

Upon a signal from Mas' Henley, Waith lit a match and the tutor's books went up in flames. At the same time, Waith slapped the horse, and the buggy lurched forward, down the drive. It was a strange sight, not unlike the first day I'd seen Mr Harms, coming up the drive of Belmont. I was sorry to see him go, but happy he was alive to go.

Sunday, January 8, 1860

Aunt Tee made me tell her what happened at least ten times. Each time when we get to the part about Spicy being hit, she says, "Bless you, chile." Spicy's eye's swollen, but Aunt Tee is taking care of her.

"How do you get brave?" I asked Spicy.

"I hope I was as brave as you are smart. It was your idea. All I did was do what you told me to do — even though I was scared to death the whole time."

Later

Missy can't stop talking about what a bad girl Spicy is. "Hince won't want a girl like that." If Missy only knew.

Monday, January 9, 1860

There is no cold like January cold. It goes through to the bone. No fire is hot enough to warm the January chills. That's what the field hands spend their time doing in January – looking for something to eat and a warm place to eat it. Most of the little children in the Quarters don't have shoes or warm clothes. Mothers come to Aunt Tee's cabin to get salves and root potions. I been working hard in the kitchen and the Big House, slipping out food a-plenty.

Tuesday, January 10, 1860

Miz Lilly called me to her room today. Jumped right on me – talking about why I didn't tell her about Spicy and Mr Harms.

"I didn't know."

She took my shoulders in each hand. Then she sighed. "Clotee, you could be my pet, my favourite, if you let me.

You're so bright and pretty just like your mama. Did you know, we were best friends? – always laughing and laughing, like silly girls do. Then we got all grown-up . . . She made the most lovely gowns for me and my sisters."

"Then you let her go." God, help me to keep my mouth.

Miz Lilly eyed me hard. "Go on now, get out of here," she said. "You're useless."

Wednesday, January 11, 1860

True to his word, Mas' Henley freed Hince today. I sneaked paper out of the study while dusting a while back. So, I've made a copy of the way a free paper is made up, and I got a copy of Mas' Henley's sign'ture. Hince can't leave though, because Mas' Henley say the papers have to be took to the courthouse.

Sunday

Now that Mr Harms is gone and we don't have no more study time, I don't know what the date is. But today is Sunday.

Missy done made sure everybody in the Quarters thinks Spicy is a bad girl. Hince staying his distance for a spell. As long as Hince and Spicy know the truth, that's all that matters.

Aunt Tee's pot is mighty low. Not enough to make a meal for us, never mind anybody else. Still she tries. Sharing what we got. "This plantation makes us all kin," she say. "Not by blood, but by suffering."

January cold

My fingers are cold. My feet are cold. My nose is cold. I cough all the time. My head hurts. This is the coldest winter of my life. I stay by the fire, but I'm never warm.

In the room over the kitchen it was always warm and comfortable. I sleep in a fit and wake up tired. I will speak to Miz Lilly about getting some of the old blankets in the upstairs room of the Big House.

Everybody gathered around Aunt Tee tonight. They seem to find hope in her spirit to keep going. Somebody sang –

Rabbits in the briar patch,
Squirrel in the tree,
Wish I could go hunting
But I ain't free.
Rooster's in the henhouse
Hen's in the patch,
Love to go shooting
But I ain't free.

"We going to eat tomorrow," say Aunt Tee. "Don't you worry."

Next day

Most times Miz Lilly is cold and mean. Today, she found a little kind piece hidden away in a pocket of her heart. I told her how bad it was in the Quarters. "It has been a bad winter." She let us take quilts and shirts and shoes down to the Quarters. Boxes of stuff. It was like the Big Times all over again.

While Miz Lilly was busy helping me in the attic, Aunt Tee slipped and rung the necks of two hens and had them in the pot with dumplings before anybody could say "how-do you do." Aunt Tee was good on her word. We ate good tonight.

Day or so later

My head hurts. My arms and legs hurt. Even my teeth hurt. I can't write any more.

Early February

I don't know what day of the week it is. They tell me I've been sick with an awful fever. Aunt Tee and Spicy used teas and salves – but it was Mama's love that pulled me through.

Whilst I was in a fever, dreaming, Mama come to me all soft and gentle. "Get well, daughter. Live and grow strong." Then she told me something that's really got me studying on the meaning. She say something Rufus used to always say, "To the one God gives much, much is asked in return." Then I saw Rufus standing with Mama. He say, "You have been given much, Clotee. You can read and write, when others can't. Now, you must put your learning to good use. Use your learning."

Use it to do what?

Week later

I'm feeling better every day. Still wobbly. I'm back working in the kitchen and Big House.

After the dishes were done from the midday meal, I walked to the woods. It's not nearly as cold as it has been. Most of the snow is melted. I passed the cemetery and spent a minute with Uncle Heb, and I remembered Rufus and Aggie, Wook and Baby Noah who never got a chance to live. Then I moved down toward the river.

I wrote F-R-E-E-D-O-M in the mud. It still has no picture. Maybe my dream meant that I should run to freedom up in the Philadelphia, the New York or the Boston, and then use my reading and writing to help the abolitionists. Is that what I should do, Mama? How would I run away?

Monday

I know it's Monday because Miz Lilly come to the kitchen to pass out the flour, sugar and meal. She gave Missy a pretty scarf to wear on her head. Then she swished past me with her head in the air. Suddenly I got an understanding. Miz Lilly is like a spoiled, silly girl – playing silly games with people's lives. She's like a little girl in a big woman's body. Pitiful.

Tuesday

It's a winter thaw. Day was almost warm. But Aunt Tee say it's a fooler. I wandered down to the spot where I had seen Mr Harms talking to the one-eyed man. No reason. Just did.

I heard the crackle of leaves underfoot. I stopped, stood dead still, listening, waiting – for what I didn't know.

"Clotee. Over here. It's me, Mr Harms."

I was sure glad to see Mr Harms and I told him so. He wondered why I had come to that place just then. "I don't know, sir. I just came." I'll always b'lieve Mama guided me there. "I thought you would be in the Boston by now," I said.

"No," he said, laughing. "But this is my last run. My partner and I are too well-known in the Tidewater. I'll move on after we take the next group out."

"Who will be the conductor here at Belmont?" I asked him.

"We won't have a conductor here. That's too bad. Belmont is an important link in the railroad."

The abolitionists will find someone, won't they?

I pulled myself tall. "Sir, I want to go with you to freedom. I'll work hard and help the abolitionists in any way I can. Please say I can come."

"Clotee, you don't have to beg. Of course you can come. Be here on the next dark of the moon. Bring fresh water but travel light – bring only what you need. It is a dangerous journey, Clotee. But you are no stranger to danger. You are a remarkable girl, and we abolitionists will be proud to have you in our ranks."

Mr Harms hugged me. "Take care, little Clotee. Thank Spicy for what she did. I have a feeling you were in on it, too." I nodded. "Tell Hince I hold no hard feelings. In his shoes I might have done the same thing." Then, "If possible, find some way to say thank you to William."

Wednesday

I've told Aunt Tee and Spicy about seeing Mr Harms and how he was planning another runaway on the next dark of the moon. But as hard as I try, I can't get Aunt Tee to go with me. Spicy wants to go, though, because Hince is going to be leaving soon as his papers clear.

"I'm too old, chile," say Aunt Tee. "Besides, I can't leave Uncle Heb. I lived with him. I'll be buried 'side of him, too. But you go on, honey. Go to that freedom here on earth."

Going without Aunt Tee? That would be like losing Mama again.

Next day

The Campbelles came to Belmont on their way back to the Deep South. "We've come for our property," said Silas Campbelle.

"He's a free man," said Mas' Henley.

I must have polished all the brass off the mas'er's doorknob trying to hear what was being said.

"You had no right to sell what didn't belong to you."

"Take me to court," said Mas' Henley.

"We'll do just that." said the Campbelles and they stormed out of the house.

Now what do we do?

Monday again

Since Mr Harms got run away, Miz Lilly been trying to teach William so he can get into Overton School. Unteach is better to say. William won't have none of it. He gets about nicely with two canes. Pretty soon, he'll be walking without them.

When William saw me watching from the hallway, he waved. Later, I stopped by his room. He was playing with Shadow.

"If Mr Harms had had time, he would have said thank you," I said.

"I'm sure he would have," said William.

I think the message got through.

Week later

I write this with a heavy heart. The judge ruled that Hince was not free because he didn't b'long to Mas' Henley when he freed him. "The free papers he wrote aine worth a lame horse."

The Campbelles are coming to get Hince Monday-week on their way back south. I've cried dry. Aunt Tee and Spicy have, too. We got to stop crying and start thinking.

Monday (I hope)

Just when you get to thinking that times can't get no worse, something else happens. The weather's like that, too – fooled us into believing spring was almost here, but it snowed again today, all day.

While I was dusting Mas' Henley's study, I come across a paper that say he was selling Spicy to a man named Mobile, Alabama. They are coming for her on Tuesday-week.

Spicy and Hince say they won't be separated – rather be dead first. Talk like that makes a cold chill go up my back.

"What we gon' do?" Spicy asked me, right pitiful-like. "You the one had the idea that saved Mr Harms. Can't you think of a way to help me and Hince?"

There are abolitionists and conductors on the underground railroad who want to help us – but we aine got time to wait on them. This time, we got to do it ourselves. We got to make an 'scape plan.

Saturday

I was reading Spicy's Bible when I turned to a page where somebody had written, "My baby girl was born on February 28, 1844."

I showed it to Spicy. "Mama must'a wrote that in the Bible," she say, touching the words with her fingers. "She could read and write like you, Clotee."

"Like you, too, Spicy. You done learned how to write your name and lots of words. With a little more practicing you'll be writing real good."

"My mama wanted to name me Rose," Spicy said.

I wrote in Spicy's Bible, Spicy's real name is Rose.

"Do you believe that everything in the Bible is true?" I asked. She nodded. "I wrote your real name in your Bible. The name your mama wanted you to be called. ROSE. From now on you are Rose."

Shortly after midnight, Sunday morning

There is a terrible thunderstorm raging outside. We had to call off the run. But we have to go no later than tomorrow.

Monday

I put my plan to work at first light. We dressed Spicy as a boy slave. I gave her a bundle. "It's our quilt," I told her. "You should keep it." She didn't have time to fuss with me about it.

Hince looks so much like a white man, we dressed him in one of Mas' Henley old suits I sneaked out of the attic. "I aine never had on a suit of clothes before," he said. We tucked Spicy's Bible under his arm. "You look like a for-real preaching man," said Aunt Tee, hugging them both and giving them a biscuit and water for a day.

Time to go. "You know what to do, now?"

Just as we planned, we slipped down to the barn, Hince mounted Big Can. Being very careful not to make a sound, I eased them through the woods, past the cemetery, toward the river. I had already done my hugging and farewelling, so I just watched them ride downstream along the bank until they was out of sight.

I slipped back on the other side of the orchards, into the cabin where Aunt Tee and I sat holding each other until dawn. By then I had stopped trembling.

Tuesday

Hince and Spicy wasn't missed until the Campbelles come for Hince on Monday. Mas' Henley crashed into Aunt Tee's cabin, wanting us to tell him where Hince and Spicy had gone.

Aunt Tee stayed calm. "We don't know a thing 'bout that. We all went to sleep together and when we woke up same as you, they was gone."

"I don't believe a word, you're saying. I don't trust any of you," he shouted and carried on.

The Campbelles didn't seem too upset. "We'll take Canterbury's Watch, then." But when they went to get the horse it, too, was gone. Then the Campbelles say that Mas' Henley was trying to cheat them. They say they was gon' take him to court.

Mas' Henley went to talking fast. "I'll pay you for your losses," he said, adding, "and for whatever inconven – (whatever that big word was) I may have caused you."

"Cash," said Silas Campbelle. "No marker."

Long 'bout that time, the slavers come for Spicy. "The boy and gal have run away," Mas' Henley told them. He had to pay the slavers back their money for Spicy.

I was beside myself with joy – joy in the morning. Serves him good. William and Miz Lilly came out on the porch. People from the Quarters were also gathering to see what was going on. Miz Lilly swooned, but nobody bothered to catch her when she fainted.

Mas' Henley and Waith set out to find Spicy and Hince but they are long gone. I was as happy as Daniel and David all in one.

Next day

I studied the sun today. It's different. I feel that winter is almost over. We will have more cold days, but the bitter times are over. We've made it through – in more ways than one.

Next day

Mas' Henley come back after a search saying he had found and killed both Spicy and Hince. He showed no proof. Besides, where was Big Can? If he'd really caught them, he'd have brought back the horse, for sure. I don't believe him. I won't believe him. Spicy and Hince made it. If they hadn't, I'd feel it.

Day later

The Dark of the Moon is coming. It will be time for me to make my run to freedom. I should be happy. I'm an abolitionist and I want to end slavery. I can't do that being a slave on a plantation. Can I?

Later

Mr Harms says there's no conductor on the Underground Railroad here at Belmont. If this station closes, what will happen to the runaways coming through here? Some might get caught. Some might get drowned like Rufus, Aggie, Wook and Baby Noah. But if they had somebody here to help them – to show them the way. . .

Later

This station can't close.

Dark of the moon

A moonless night is scary, 'specially in the woods when it's cloudy.

I sang the Underground Railroad song – the one Mr Harms said to signal him with.

Deep river, Lord. I want to cross over

Mr Harms met me as planned, rising up out of the darkness like a ghost. I felt better when I saw the runaways huddled together, fearing what was behind, fearing what was in front of them.

"Spicy and Hince aine going," I say, telling him how I'd helped them to get away.

"I've heard 'bout their getaway." Mr Harms already knew about it?

"Have you heard if they safe?" My heart was pounding from wondering and worrying. I rather know a bad thing than to not know it.

"Our conductors tell me Spicy and Hince are in northern waters on their way to Canada. Where'd you come up with such a good idea?" he asked, smiling.

It seemed easy enough to me. Hince passed as a white man, travelling with his slave. When they got to Richmond, Hince sold Canterbury's Watch – to a kind man who will give Can a good home. I had made out the papers to show the horse had been sold to Hince Henley, a cousin of Mas' Henley's. I'd copied his signature, too.

Hince used the money to buy tickets on the first steamship heading north, just like I told him.

"Some of our people who were on the boat said Hince had won a large amount of money gambling with a group of wealthy young men who found him quite charming." I can just see him now, teasing, smiling. They never suspected he was a runaway slave.

"Now it's time to get you out of here, Clotee," said Mr Harms.

"Have you found a person to be the conductor here at Belmont?"

"No we haven't."

"I'm not going with you, now. I want to stay here and be a conductor on the Underground Railroad at this station."

Next night

I didn't sleep last night and when I did it was fitful. Had I done the right thing? I kept seeing Mama's face. She was smiling and that made me feel better.

Mr Harms made me promise to meet him at the river again tonight. I did.

"It is too dangerous for you to be a conductor," said Mr Harms. "You're just a child."

"I'm young, sir, all due respect, but I'm not a child," I told him. "I'm an abolitionist. And I'm needed. Anyway, it was my idea that saved you from the sheriff. It was my plan that got Spicy and Hince away. I can do it."

"Oh, I have no doubt that you're up to the job," said Mr Harms. "You are a remarkable young lady, and I'm proud of you. But don't you want to be free?"

I had talked this over with myself long and hard, so I knew what I felt. "Yes sir, I want to be free. But most of all I want slavery to end for everybody. I read in one of your papers that it's not right for anybody to be slaves. So, that's why I want to stay – to make an end to slavery."

Mr Harms looked surprised and pleased. "You have a better understanding of freedom than most people do," said Mr Harms. It was my time to look surprised. "Freedom is about making choices and learning from them," he said. "You've made the choice to stay here. The conductor's job is yours as long as you want it. But remember," he added, "the first sign of trouble you must get out of here. Promise?" I promised.

Into March

We are turning the ground for the new crop – back-breaking work. I'm not as afraid as I once was. I don't let my fear stop me from my work. I've started teaching a few trusted slaves to write. It's scary, because I know if they are ever really put to a hard test, they will probably turn me in. But I can't worry about that now. If I don't teach them, who will?

Miz Lilly has put me in the fields. I'm happy here, because I'm making more and more choices. I see why Spicy wanted to be out here, away from Miz Lilly and Mas' Henley who are mean as ever. So is Waith.

Since Spicy and Hince ran away, Waith's been very hard

on us. We try not to give him reasons to beat us, but he still finds them. When it's time for me to teach school or when it's time for a runaway, we know how to handle Waith. See, he took a liking to Aunt Tee's root tea, so we just put a little sleeping herb in Waith's tea. He never knows the difference.

Sunday

Without us even noticing it, spring has pushed up everywhere. Easter came and went. We will celebrate Aunt Tee's birthday.

The orchards bloomed weeks ago. No late frost got them, so we'll have a good crop of apples this year. Uncle Heb's garden is in bloom. Mas' Henley finally realized how much work it takes to keep Belmont grounds looking beautiful.

April 1860

I haven't written in a long time ... one month, maybe. Since I'm not in the Big House, it's hard for me to get paper to add to my diary. But I can scratch in the dirt, and I do. Practising and teaching others.

William is going off to school in Missouri, and Miz Lilly is trying to die, because it aine Overton. I got a feeling that boy was really 'fected by Mr Harms, more than anybody will ever know – other than me. Who knows, William might end up being an abolitionist. Now wouldn't that take the cake?

Mas' Henley finally got tired of eating Eva Mae's bad cooking. He sent her back to the fields, then brought in a new cook from New Orleans. Uses lots of peppers. Nobody will ever be as good as Aunt Tee at cooking fried chicken and whipped potatoes. And he knows it.

Miz Lilly has made Missy her pet. Missy don't speak and never comes to the Quarters not even to see her mama. Missy wears all kinds of pretty dresses but she can't be too happy – not living under Miz Lilly day after day.

Aunt Tee is busy all the time – picking wild greens, making potions, birthing babies – and helping me make plans for runaways. A group will be passing through Belmont in a few days.

Full moon, April, 1860

Aunt Tee sang the signal –

Swing low, sweet chariot,
Coming for to carry me home

A group of three runaways found their way to the Belmont station tonight. One of them was a girl about ten. She was so scared. I pressed Little Bit in her hand. "She will keep you company," I said. The girl managed a weak smile. I had their passes written. Aunt Tee had their food and water ready.

Soon, a man dressed in black rowed up to the bank, making not a splash with his oars. "Come quickly." He was my partner, but we'd never talked or seen each other. Safer that way. He sounded like a foreigner. "See you next time," he said. I never saw his face. Quickly and quietly the runaways got in the boat and rowed away. I don't think I took a breath until they were out of sight.

Sitting here next to Aunt Tee in the cabin I feel good about staying for now. One day I'll see the Philadelphia, the New York and the Boston. Maybe I'll make my own run for freedom next year – or maybe the next. Until then I have plenty of work to do.

Next day

I have just enough paper and berry ink to write one more time.

The morning bell will ring soon and I'll have to go to the fields. There's time to write a few words. I have decided to begin with F-R-E-E-D-O-M. Freedom. I let the memory pictures take shape in my mind. Mr Harms is safe and able to go on with his work. Hince and Spicy are free and together. I remembered the little girl I'd helped the night before and I smiled. My doll Little Bit would be free before me. Freedom. I remembered what Mr Harms had said about choices. I looked at the letters more closely. For the first time freedom showed me a clear picture.

A picture of me.

Epilogue

During the summer of 1939, when Clotee Henley was 92 years old, she was interviewed by Lucille Avery, a student at Fisk University, which is in Nashville, Tennessee. Miss Avery, along with many other writers, had been hired by the government to visit aging slaves and record their stories. Clotee's story first appeared in the *Virginia Chronicle*, summer 1940.

Miss Avery visited Clotee at her home in Hampton, Virginia. And for over two months, Clotee shared her diaries, photos and papers. From Miss Avery's research, we know that Clotee served as a conductor on the Underground Railroad, helping over 150 slaves get to freedom, and as a spy for the Union Army from 1862 – 1865. She was awarded a commendation by General Ulysses S Grant for her valour.

During the war however, life at Belmont changed forever. Briley Waith was at Fort Sumter with Edmund Ruffin, Sr, who fired the first shot. Mas' Henley lost an arm at the battle of Fredericksburg, and Miz Lilly went mad when Yankees camped on Belmont grounds and turned the Big House into a Union hospital. Aunt Tee used all her knowledge of roots and herbs to save the lives of soldiers, even when army doctors snickered and called it voodoo. They stopped laughing when she saved more lives than they did. Sadly, Aunt Tee died of cholera on Christmas Day 1864, months before the war ended. She was buried beside Uncle Heb in the plantation cemetery. When Missy's mama died, she ran off and later married a Buffalo Soldier out West.

After the war, Mr Harms arranged for Clotee to travel up North, where she received a hero's welcome. After several business failures, Mr Harms moved to Scotland where he dropped out of sight. Although Clotee never met Sojourner Truth, she did meet Frederick Douglass, with whom she corresponded until his death in 1895.

In 1875, Clotee returned to Virginia, where she attended Virginia Colored Women's Institute, then dedicated her life to the education of former slaves, women's suffrage, equal rights and justice for all people regardless of race, creed or nationality.

Inside her diaries, Miss Avery found two other interesting items that help conclude Clotee's story. One was a photo and packet of letters from Dr William Monroe Henley, who had become a professor of philosophy at Oberlin College in Ohio. He had been disinherited by his father for taking a stand against prejudice. "Through education Mr Harms did more to destroy slavery than all the laws on the books could legislate," he wrote to Clotee in 1891.

There was another photo of a handsome elderly couple, surrounded by a large family. On the back was written: To our beloved sister-friend, Clotee from Hince and Rose Henley and family. 50th Wedding Anniversary. Louisville, Kentucky, 1910.

Spicy is holding a Bible in her hand, and Hince has a quilt folded over one knee. There is an old article from a Kentucky newspaper attached to the photo, praising Hince for being one of the finest horse trainers in the racing business.

Clotee never married or had children of her own, but when she died on May 6, 1941, hundreds of her former students attended the funeral. As a teacher she had challenged them. As an activist, she had inspired them. As a friend, she had encouraged them. Clotee Henley's legacy lives on in the epitaph engraved on her gravestone:

FREEDOM IS MORE THAN A WORD

Historical note

The first Africans were brought to the Virginia colony as indentured servants in 1619. Slavery was a well-established institution in the United States by the 1850s. But the resistance against it was equally old and persistent.

Virginia legislators, who were often wealthy planters, took the lead in passing laws that safeguarded their rights as slaveholders, discouraged runaways and protected themselves against insurrections. These laws were known as "Slave Codes" or "Black Codes". As a matter of record Virginia and other Southern states had hundreds of Slave Codes on their books. For example one stated that "...the status of the mother determined whether the child was born free or slave." Others forbade interracial marriages and outlawed the education of slaves. Blacks could not hold public meetings, or testify against a white man in court. Any slave suspected of running away was dealt with severely.

Resistance against slavery took many forms, beginning first with the captives themselves. They used work slow downs, arson, murder, suicide and armed rebellion to gain their freedom. When they could run, most did. In fact, the runaway problem was always a pressing one for most slaveholders. As early as 1642, Virginia introduced a fugitive slave order that penalized all those who helped runaway slaves.

Even the United States Constitution contained a fugitive slave clause. Most slaves who managed to reach a free state could live as a free person. But with the passage of the revised Fugitive Slave Law of 1850, the government allowed slaveholders to go into free states and recapture their "property".

In 1854, Anthony Burns, a fugitive slave, was arrested and jailed in Boston, Massachusetts, but Bostonians attacked the federal courthouse and attempted to rescue him. Burns was returned to his master, but he was later freed. Burns' case, and others like his, brought the issue of slavery to the forefront.

As early as 1688, a group of Pennsylvania Quakers signed the "Germantown Mennonite Resolution Against Slavery". It was the first written document that protested slavery in the North American colonies and marked the beginning of a formalized abolitionist movement. Since that time, blacks and whites, men and women, southerners and northerners organized with the purpose of abolishing slavery. One of the largest and most effective of these organizations was the American Anti-Slavery Society, founded in Philadelphia in 1833. New York, Philadelphia and Boston were the centres of the movement, but anti-slavery groups flourished all over the country.

William Lloyd Garrison and Frederick Douglass spoke out strongly against slavery. Women such as Harriet Beecher Stowe and Sojourner Truth also made an impact through their lectures and writing. Truth had been enslaved in New York, one of the last Northern states to abolish slavery. Stowe's book *Uncle Tom's Cabin* sold out its first printing in less than a week because people were fascinated by her depiction of slave life. Southerners tried to argue that the book was fiction, but people read it as fact.

To help runaways make the long and dangerous trip to freedom, often to Canada, abolitionists formed a network of people who served as "conductors" on an "underground railroad". It was not underground and it wasn't a railroad, but a route by which slaves were taken to freedom. Good and decent people – farmers, teachers, housewives, labourers, college presidents and even children – risked heavy fines and imprisonment to take part in this dangerous venture. Some conductors were caught and served time in prison but nothing could stop people from running away from tyranny or assisting those who would try.

One of the best-known conductors on the Underground Railroad was Harriet Tubman, a fugitive slave. Although there was a price on her head, she continued to serve as a conductor, leading hundreds of runaways to freedom in Canada.

Slaveholders had their sights on the fertile lands out West. They wanted to expand slavery west of the Mississippi River.

Abolitionists were determined to stop them. Dred Scott, a Missouri slave, sued his master for freedom because he had been taken to live for a while in free territory. The United States Supreme Court ruled in 1857 that a slave could not sue for his freedom because he was "property". The court added that "no black man had rights that a white man [had] to respect." The decision was a bitter defeat for anti-slavery forces, because it disenfranchised all blacks – whether free or slave. Now, neither could vote, hold public office, patent an invention, serve on a jury or testify against a white person in any court of law. African Americans were not considered citizens.

While most abolitionists chose to end slavery through peaceful means, some were beginning to think that slavery could not end without an armed struggle. Henry Highland Garnet was an outspoken black leader who called for violent resistance to slavery long before anyone else agreed with him. Another man who believed that freedom would have to be won by the sword was John Brown.

In October 1859, John Brown, along with five blacks and thirteen whites, led a raid on the federal armoury at Harpers Ferry in Virginia (now located in West Virginia). Brown planned to organize a slave army made up of fugitives who would fight for their own freedom. Their success would inspire others to take up arms. Colonel Robert E Lee led the federal counterattack. Most of Brown's men were killed in the fight. One man escaped. John Brown and several others were captured and hanged. Before he died, Brown warned the South to end slavery or risk God's wrath.

To anti-slavery sympathizers Brown had become a hero, a martyr. Songs were written about him and schoolchildren honoured him. In the South, Brown was dismissed as a madman, symbolic of all abolitionists.

The South was confident in 1859 that their way of life would go on indefinitely. But change was inevitable. The Republicans were a new political party, organized in 1854. In less than five years they had won numerous seats in Congress. Abraham Lincoln from Illinois was nominated to run for the presidency on the Republican ticket. He stood a fair chance of winning the 1860 election. His position seemed moderate, nothing radical. He supported Congressional prohibition of slavery in Western territories and the gradual abolition of slavery in the United States. Some abolitionist groups felt Lincoln's position was not strong enough. Some leaders, especially in Virginia, realized that slavery could not last much longer and the gradual approach seemed plausible. Sadly, these people were in the minority. South Carolina declared that if Lincoln won the election, the state would secede from the Union.

Meanwhile political posturing had done very little to ease the lives of the 4,000,000 slaves who lived on the plantations throughout the South. Most of them lived in miserable conditions, yet they never lost hope. It is reflected in the songs they sang:

Swing low, sweet chariot,
Comin' for to carry me home.
A band of angels comin' after me.
Comin' for to carry me home.

The words were coded. "Home" was freedom. The "sweet chariot" was a wagon or some vehicle that they hoped would take them to freedom. The "band of angels" were the abolitionists. Slaves sang songs for many reasons. Often, their singing was misunderstood as a display of happiness and contentment.

The conditions under which a slave lived depended largely upon the personality of his master. Planters were the masters of their estates who conducted their affairs autonomously. Their wives, children and slaves were under their authority and could be treated any way the planters chose within the limits of the law (and the laws were always in the slaveholders' favour).

The mistress of the plantation was generally younger than her husband, sometimes by as much as twenty years. Girls often married at fourteen and were expected to have children as soon as possible. But the rearing of the children was usually left to slave women who nursed and cared for them through infancy.

The master's children grew up on the plantation and sometimes played with slave children because there were no other children around. Sometimes slave children were half brothers and sisters, sharing the same father. Loneliness caused some mistresses to select a slave woman to be her confidante and companion. The relationship was rarely allowed to develop into real friendship. Each situation was as unique as the people who were involved.

In 1859 most slaveholders owned no more than 25 to 30 field hands and four to five household servants who took care of the family's personal needs. Field slaves' lives were filled with endless misery and suffering. Death was welcomed. They worked from sunup until sundown, driven by fear and brutality. Their diets were poor, and so was their health care. People aged early and died too young. Children died needless deaths and the elderly were turned out to fend for themselves when they were no longer useful. The huts the slaves lived in were small, crowded and filthy, and up to as many as ten people would sleep in one 6 metre by 6 metre cabin.

Those servants who worked in the "Big House" had a few advantages, but there were even more disadvantages. As grand as the old mansions were, they didn't have any of the modern conveniences we take for granted today. Work in the Big House never ceased. Servants were expected to do all the washing, ironing, cooking, serving of food, cleaning, caring for children and even fanning. House slaves were on call 24 hours a day.

Even though every effort was made to keep slaves ignorant, many of them learned to read and write, using any opportunity available to them. Then they, in turn, taught others. Secret teachers – who were sometimes disguised abolitionists, free blacks or fellow slaves – formed "pit schools". They dug a hole large enough for two to four people. They pulled a lid made of brush over the top. Down in the pit they practised their lessons with less chance of being caught.

Being discovered was an ever-present danger. Literate slaves were usually sold to the Deep South where escape was nearly impossible. Gabriel Prosser and Nat Turner were literate men who had led rebellions in Richmond and Southampton, Virginia. Slaveowners knew they were outnumbered on some rural plantations, so masters stayed on the lookout for budding insurrections. They used bribery, threats and fear to coerce slaves into betraying anyone who might appear suspicious. It was not uncommon for the informer to end up being sold himself.

Frederick Douglass, publisher of *The North Star*, wrote in his autobiography that "No man who can read will stay a slave very long."

Sojourner Truth, who had been a slave in New York, said, "Slavery must be destroyed. God will not stand with wrong, never mind how right you think you be."

And Harriet Tubman said, "I mean to live free or die."

Emboldened by the spirit of these and other freedom

fighters, the stage was set for slaves who dared to defy their masters.

People didn't know in 1859 that the nation was on the threshold of a terrible war that would kill thousands. But the unfolding political drama would climax when Edmund Ruffin, Sr, a Virginian, fired the first shot at Fort Sumter, South Carolina, a few months after Abraham Lincoln was elected President of the United States. The war ended five years later in 1865. The cost had been high on both sides. The lives of the 4,000,000 slaves living in the United States and the 250,000 fugitive slaves that had escaped to Canada would be changed forever.

They were free at last.

The cabins in the slave quarters could be as small as 4 metres square. They were made of wood with dirt floors and windows without panes. They had to accommodate about ten to twelve people.

A pass for the Underground Railroad. It reads: "My Dear Mrs Post: Please shelter this Sister from the house of bondage till five o'clock – this afternoon – She will then be sent on to the land of freedom. Yours truly, Fred K." Fred K. was Frederick Douglass, the famous escaped slave. He became a well-known lecturer and founded the abolitionist newspaper, *The North Star*.

$200 Reward.

RANAWAY from the subscriber, on the night of Thursday, the 30th of Sepember,

FIVE NEGRO SLAVES,

To-wit : one Negro man, his wife, and three children.

The man is a black negro, full height, very erect, his face a little thin. He is about forty years of age, and calls himself *Washington Reed*, and is known by the name of Washington. He is probably well dressed, possibly takes with him an ivory headed cane, and is of good address. Several of his teeth are gone.

Mary, his wife, is about thirty years of age, a bright mulatto woman, and quite stout and strong.

The oldest of the children is a boy, of the name of FIELDING, twelve years of age, a dark mulatto, with heavy eyelids. He probably wore a new cloth cap.

MATILDA, the second child, is a girl, six years of age, rather a dark mulatto, but a bright and smart looking child.

MALGOLM, the youngest, is a boy, four years old, a lighter mulatto than the last, and about equally as bright. He probably also wore a cloth cap. If examined, he will be found to have a swelling at the navel. Washington and Mary have lived at or near St. Louis, with the subscriber, for about 15 years.

It is supposed that they are making their way to Chicago, and that a white man accompanies them, that they will travel chiefly at night, and, most probably in a covered wagon.

A reward of $150 will be paid for their apprehension, so that I can get them, if taken within one hundred miles of St. Louis, and $300 if taken beyond that, and secured so that I can get them, and other reasonable additional charges, if delivered to the subscriber, or to THOMAS ALLEN, Esq., at St. Louis, Mo. The above negroes, for the last few years, have been in possession of Thomas Allen, Esq., of St. Louis.

WM. RUSSELL.

ST. LOUIS, Oct 1, 1847.

Posters announcing a reward for the capture and return of runaway slaves were very common.

Work in the fields was gruelling, and slaves rarely had enough to eat to sustain them through the long, exhausting days.

Harriet Tubman was the most famous conductor on the Underground Railroad. A runaway slave from Maryland, she made about twenty trips from the North into the South and rescued more than 300 slaves.

A freed slave, Sojourner Truth was one of the most famous abolitionists and activists for the rights of blacks and women. Although she was illiterate, Truth could quote the Bible word for word and was a powerful and affecting preacher.

Go Down, Moses

Words and music to "Go Down, Moses". While slaveowners believed religion had a placating effect on slaves, the Bible and its stories were a great source of strength and inspiration to seek freedom. In this traditional negro spiritual, the slaves identified with the Jews of Egypt who were also held in bondage by the cruel Pharaoh. Harriet Tubman was said to be the Moses of the slaves' song, helping runaway slaves escape from "Egypt's land".

Picture acknowledgments

Grateful acknowledgment is made for permission to reprint the following:

P 222 (top)   Slave cabin, The Library of Congress

P 222 (bottom) Pass for the Underground Railroad, Department of Rare Books and Special Collections, University of Rochester Library, Rochester, New York.

P 223 (top)   Reward poster, The Library of Congress

P 223 (bottom) Cotton pickers, ibid

P 224   Harriet Tubman, The Library of Congress

P 225   Sojourner Truth, The Library of Congress

P 226   Words and music to "Go Down, Moses", from Songs of the Civil War, Dover Publications, Inc., New York, New York

Experience history first-hand with *My Story* –
a series of vividly imagined accounts of life in the past.

It's 1935 and Eleanor and her best friend, Sarah, are
determined to compete in the national swimming team for
the 1936 Olympics. Their dream comes true when both are
selected. But the host city is Hitler's Berlin and
Sarah is Jewish.

Eleanor witnesses the Nazi's hostility to Jews and hears the
distant murmurings that will erupt into WWII.

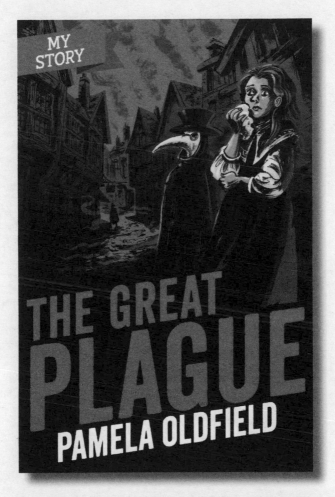

It's 1665 and Alice is excited to be back in her beloved
London. But the plague is spreading, and each day more red
crosses mark the doors of the sick. When her aunt becomes
ill, Alice is forced to make a decision that could change her
life forever.

But will she be able to get the papers that allow her to leave?
Will she be able to find safety away from home?

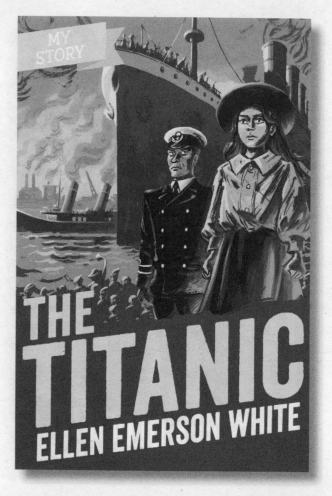

MY STORY

THE TITANIC
ELLEN EMERSON WHITE

Margaret Anne can't believe her luck when she's chosen to accompany Mrs Carstairs on board the great ship, Titanic. But when she's woken on a freezing night in April 1912, Margaret Anne finds herself caught up in an unimaginable nightmare.

Will she be able to get to a lifeboat in time?
Will Robert?

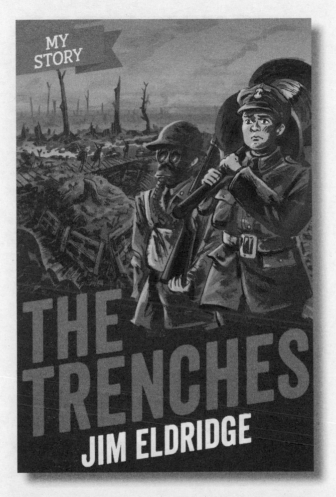

It's 1917 and Billy Stevens is a telegraph operator stationed near Ypres. The Great War has been raging for three years when Billy finds himself taking part in the deadly Big Push forward.

Will he and his friends be able to survive, especially after discovering that the bullets of their fellow soldiers aren't just aimed at the enemy?

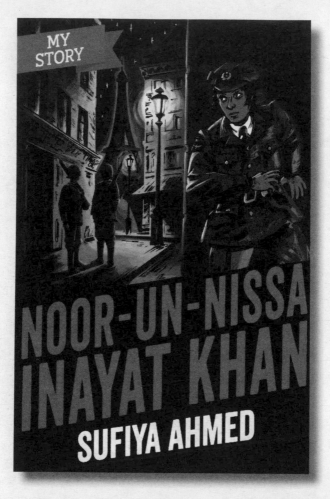

MY STORY

NOOR-UN-NISSA INAYAT KHAN

SUFIYA AHMED

It's 1940 and hundreds of families are fleeing Nazi-occupied France before it's too late. Noor and her family leave Paris for England, where she signs up to the Women's Auxiliary Air Force (WAAF) against her mother's wishes.

Noor returns to France, but this time as a secret agent. Can she keep her true identity hidden, report her findings back to London and help the Allies win the war?

MY STORY

BLITZ

VINCE CROSS

It's 1940 and Edie is being evacuated to Wales along with her brother, Tom. Far from home and missing her family, Edie is determined to be strong, but life in the countryside proves to be much tougher than it was in London.

Should Edie stick it out as her parents would want, or do something to protect her little brother?

MY STORY

THE MAYFLOWER

KATHRYN LASKY

It's 1620 and Remember (Mem) and her family have survived
the gruelling sea voyage and reached the New World. Despite
bad conditions, Mem is fearless – she helps care for the sick
and wants more than anything to settle into her new home.

Will she be able to do so with her
friends and family?

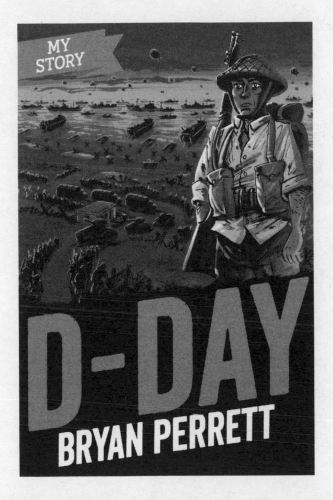

MY STORY

D-DAY

BRYAN PERRETT

It's 1944 when Lieutenant Andy Pope takes part in the D-Day landings, crossing the English Channel to the beaches of Normandy. Ordered to cut off the Germans' line of retreat, Andy's company comes under sustained attack.

When he finds himself the only unwounded officer left, will he be able to do what it takes to command his men and fight for survival?